"*History's Fiction* (title) is perfect: memorable and fitting . . . It's so perfect that it may also capture the spirit of her novels - *Unwalled City* and *Hong Kong Rose,* which chronicle Hong Kong's history through fickle fiction."
— *Far Eastern Economic Review*

"Here is an immensely gratifying collection of stories from a truly international writer . . . *History's Fiction* contains the kind of complexity and inter-connectedness of Hong Kong itself . . . These stories will shock and surprise you the same way a walk down Hong Kong's streets will — ordinary and extraordinary blend almost effortlessly."
— *The Asian Review of Books*

"Reading Xu Xi . . . becomes reminiscent of reading Nobel Prize Winner Gabriel Marquez's masterpieces, with their themes of eternal return . . . The book does exceed its bilingual title, and should also leave the new reader curious about her older works, and her avid reader hungry for her new works that are yet to come."
— *Quarterly Literary Review Singapore*

"Xu Xi manages to avoid the usual cliches . . . there are no taipans, no triads and no tender-hearted bar girls in these tales . . . explains the paradox that is Hong Kong."
— *South China Morning Post*

WHAT OTHER WRITERS SAY OF
HISTORY'S FICTION

"Writes of people living between places, between loves, between histories. In her stories, you usually find someone you seem to know."
— Agnes Lam, poet *Woman to Woman* and
Water, Wood, Pure Splendour

"In these stories, Xu Xi gives history a face, a voice, a heart. Her brilliant contemporary rendering paints a less exotic Hong Kong, and thus brings its people closer to our every day. These are the kind of stories that lasts, for they are as universal as the first touch of love. As a lover of excellent fiction from the faraway, I am ever so grateful for writers like Xu Xi for bringing me so close."
— Bino Realuyo, novelist *The Umbrella Country*

"Haunting. Xu Xi's delicate, probing stories mix memory and desire, weaving together East and West across time and space."
— Simon Elegant, novelist *A Floating World* and
A Chinese Wedding

"One of Hong Kong's most prominent writers does it again. Recounting the past in today's voice, her stories showcase the tension between East-West relationships, providing a compelling "history between the sheets.""
— Hwee Hwee Tan, novelist *Foreign Bodies* and *Mammon Inc.*

XU XI was born in Hong Kong to a Chinese-Indonesian family. The city was home to her until her mid-twenties, after which she led a peripatetic existence around Europe, America and Asia. For eighteen non-consecutive years, the author held a second career in international marketing and management with various multinationals. At the end of 1997, she finally surrendered completely to fiction. She now inhabits the flight path connecting New York, Hong Kong and New Zealand.

The New York Times named her a pioneer writer from Asia in English. "In the 1970's and 1980's, when she was developing her fictional voice, Xu Xi felt alone in her homeland. Unlike most Asian writers here, she wrote in English. Twice, for long periods, her antidote for isolation was to live in the United States." She is an active champion of writing from Asia, and co-edited two anthologies of Hong Kong literature in English, *City Voices* and *City Stage*. There is no question, as *Asiaweek* once said of her work, "that she gets to the heart of the matter." In addition her writing, she also teaches at the MFA program of Vermont College in Montpelier.

Awards include an O. Henry prize story, a New York State Arts Foundation fiction fellowship and the *South China Morning Post* story contest winner. She has been a resident writer at Chateau de Lavigny in Switzerland, the Jack Kerouac Project in Florida, Kulturhuset of Norway, and the Anderson Center in Minnesota. Her fiction, essays, book reviews and op-eds have been published and broadcast internationally. She holds a MFA in fiction from the University of Massachusetts at Amherst.

History's Fiction was her fifth book, and this new edition includes a reader's guide. For further information on her work and life, please visit www.xuxiwriter.com.

HISTORY'S FICTION

(2nd Edition)

A Chameleon Press book

HISTORY'S FICTION

ISBN 988-97061-2-1

© 2005 Xu Xi (*a.k.a.* S. Komala)

Published by Chameleon Press
23rd Floor, 245-251 Hennessy Road, Hong Kong
www.chameleonpress.com

Agent for all rights HAROLD MATSON COMPANY
276 Fifth Avenue, New York, NY 10001 • *hmatsco@aol.com*

Typeset in Adobe Garamond and Optima

Cover design by Image Alpha (Holdings) Ltd.

Printed and bound in Hong Kong by Regal Printing

HISTORY'S FICTION

Stories from the City of Hong Kong

by

XU XI

with a critical reading guide by
Mike Ingham

Chameleon Press

ACKNOWLEDGEMENTS

These stories, or an earlier version, were originally published as follows:

"Democracy" first appeared in *Dimsum*, **5**, Hong Kong, 2001; "Until the Next Century" first appeared in *Carve*, **2**, www.carvezine.com, 2000, and subsequently in *The Best of Carve Magazine*, Volume 2, Mild Horse Press, California, 2001; "Insignificant Moments in the History of Hong Kong" first appeared in *Dimsum*, **1**, Hong Kong, 1999; an earlier version of "Blackjack" appeared in the *South China Morning Post*, Hong Kong, 28th November, 1992 as the winning entry for the annual short story contest, and was also broadcast on RTHK, Hong Kong, 1992 (Chako); an earlier version of "The Fourth Copy or Dancing with Skeletons and Other Romances" appeared in the anthology *Home to Stay: Asian American Women's Fiction*, Greenfield Review Press, New York, 1990 (Chako); "Rage" first appeared in *The Little Magazine*, **17**, New York, 1991 (Chako); "Allegro Quasi Una Fantasia" is an excerpt from a novel manuscript, *Concerto in a Major Key*, which is archived at the library of the University of Massachusetts at Amherst, presented as a thesis for the Masters of Fine Arts in fiction, awarded 1985 (Chako); an earlier version of "The Tryst" first appeared in *Frugal Chariot*, Spring issue, Rhode Island, 1989 and subsequently in a slightly revised form in the *Hawaii Review*, **28**, 1989 (Chako); "Dannemora" first appeared in Phoebe, **4**, 2, New York, 1992 (Chako); "The Yellow Line" was first broadcast on the BBC World Service's Short Story Program, English, 1981, and subsequently in Mandarin, 1985, and was also broadcast on RTHK, English, Hong Kong, 1982; it also appeared in *Short Story International*, **36**, New York, 1991 (Komala); "Chung King Mansion" is excerpted from the novel *Chinese Walls*, Asia 2000, Hong Kong, 1994 (Chako), and subsequently in Chinese Walls & Daughters of Hui, 2nd edition, Chameleon Press, Hong Kong, 2002.

History's Fiction 1st edition, Chameleon Press, Hong Kong, 2001.

Work published prior to 1996 appeared under Xu Xi's (English) name(s).

On a summer's afternoon in '79 I watched as Susie, a slender and sexy brunette, glided over the South China Seas. She was, as always, in brilliant form. I could imagine her popping out of the startlingly blue around Dubai, her previous home, a lithe and mythic figure, balancing as she swayed.

That afternoon, as we sat anchored in Hong Kong's waters, she told me. "You must collect your stories in a book."

We were both then in our twenties, when life was resplendent with possibilities. We waterskied and confided dreams over wine, and wound up, unintentionally, sharing a lover. The sun was constantly in our eyes. Perhaps that was why for many years I could not fully realize a "collected works," blinded as I was by the idea of collection, hence losing sight of the work itself.

I no longer know where Susie is or who she married or if she is in love, or even where our lover went, meaning the man I was in love with then who loved her more. That's history.

But I am grateful to her for articulating — so easily and lightly her words flew past the wake — an idea of that which must be done.

Her imperative ascends from the morass of personal history, refusing to die, and made this collection happen.

To my English sea goddess **Susie**
and in memory of **Yang Yi Lung** (John Young)
historian, writer and friend who left us too soon,
this book is dedicated.

CONTENTS

Author's Preface

When the idea for this collection first began to gel some three years earlier, I had an unexpected creative experience. A title for the book emerged in Cantonese. At first I dismissed it, because I do not write fiction in Chinese. Although my voices speak in multiple dialects and accents, my literary "job" has been and always will be to render them in English.

Yet I could not shake the phrase. So I wrote it out, tacked it on my bulletin board, and left it there.

香 港 人 的 短 歷 史

Heunggong yahn dik duen liksi.

It became an *idée fixé*. All instincts told me it was what I was trying to say. What I wasn't sure of was its resonance.

Tentatively, almost a little fearfully, I finally decided to ask a "typical Hong Kong Chinese," if indeed such a being exists. Over *yum cha* with my friend, the poet Leung Ping-kwan who writes in both Chinese and English, I uttered the phrase. A spark ignited in his eyes and I knew, right then, the true and most important reason for this collection.

Its literal translation, "Hong Kong people's short history," does not do it justice, which was why the English title took another year to evolve. I speak to our city's history, through fiction, against the backdrop of events that marked the recent decades. What I needed to articulate was the peculiar nature of history for us *because* we were Hong Kong people, while still recognizing the universal quality of our feelings.

I eventually said the final title to another "typical" Hong

Kong person, my Sri Lankan friend Nury Vittachi, who writes only in English, although he has been known, like me, to sneak in "Chinglish" and Cantonese as well. His answer was music in any language: yes.

History, according to one definition, is *that which is not of current concern.* If that were its only meaning, this collection could not exist. I prefer the idea of history as narrative, as a chronicle of development.

As a writer, I like to believe I can and will evolve. What I published in the seventies differs from later work. However, the *concerns* of the past remain current, regardless of when a story is written.

What follows here are stories "from the city of Hong Kong," a city that remains my perpetual concern. Time and place do not define it, although moments of its history do. We do not experience history as chronicled by historians. Rather, we know where we were when the buses stopped in 1967 amid the riots on Nathan Road, or to whom we turned when midnight struck on June 30, 1997.

In compiling this collection, I looked through my fiction written over the years and saw two recurrent themes in the works that referenced my birthplace. First was an obsession with the private space of lives, how people love, despair, rejoice, confront, deny, regret, define and re-define personal existence within the boundaries of, and from a connection to, Hong Kong. The second was the intrusive quality of history in the making, most notably, the "handover."

What became clear, in thinking about all my stories, was

that historical events, whether local or larger especially *vis á vis* China, invaded all these private lives. Grey U.S. battleships color the harbor during the Vietnam War and prostitutes dye their hair orange. During the late seventies, bomb scares delay flights from Manila to Hong Kong but a woman waits till the eighties to explode. When China draws open the bamboo curtain, foreign correspondents fall in a "sort of" love with their brand of "Suzie Wongs." Meanwhile, "Tiananmen" enters our language to mean something more than the place it names. And the long awaited "millennium moment" marks the end of a longer affair, quietly, without fuss, the way history cannot.

Hence, *History's Fiction,* which emerged through these stories and others over some thirty years, selectively collected, and titled in two of our "native tongues," in order to savor, again, the taste of summer wine in Hong Kong, the city that won't let me go.

XU XI
February, 2001
Orlando, Florida

THE NINETIES

UNTIL THE NEXT CENTURY
for Rebecca Ng

"Quingfu." He handed her the chilled champagne.

She took it and kissed the tip of his nose. "Quick, close the door." Even now, she welcomed him this way, recalling the first time when, embarrassed by his presence, she wanted to pull him in, to conceal him from the neighbors.

He loosened his tie. His jacket hung untidily over his arm. "Are you well?"

"Same as usual." She hung his jacket in the closet. Long before she knew better, she would drape it on the back of a chair, thinking, there were plenty of chairs and this way, when their time was up, he could grab it and run. But he proved careless, sitting in the same chair his jacket was on, leaning against it, rumpling it further. In the end, she'd given up and put it away, out of his clumsy reach.

"It's been awhile."

How like him to be vague. "Six months."

"Shi ma?"

He had lapsed into Mandarin, but she held her tongue. Why argue anymore that reality was lived in Cantonese? Besides, Hong Kong's transformation was already well underway; their city would enter the new century as "China." "Things have changed a little." Seeing the flicker of disbelief in his eyes, she added, "it does, you know, with time."

"Time, what's time? We're forever 'young at heart,' aren't we?"

She winced. No imagination, ever. "You're almost seventy."

"Sixty eight," he corrected.

"Only for one more day." That would get him. Still the pursuit of youth. A moment's jocularity passed; the familiar irritation rose, stuck in her gullet. "Why did you want to see me?"

"Don't I always want to? Besides, who else looks after you like I do?"

The presumption! "I'm fine."

"I thought we could celebrate." When she did not respond, her face hard, he added, "you like remembering. It is our anniversary after all."

"Would have been." The words leapt out, more sharply than she intended.

"Would have been," he repeated.

They had met on a New Year's Eve, about half an hour before midnight. The party was a large one, at the home of an artistic Shanghainese family who had Westerners as friends. She came along reluctantly with a girlfriend, her classmate from university. Her own upbringing was strict. Had her parents known she were consorting with such cosmopolitan types, from Shanghai to boot, she would have hell to pay. She was nineteen.

"Remember how I kissed you?" The quaver in his voice interrupted.

"Only because I let you."

"You were my first Southern girl." Because he was originally from Beijing, having escaped, nine years earlier in '49, alone.

"But you've kissed others since."

"No, only you, my *Gwongdung* love."

They had held this conversation many times, improvising variations to amuse themselves. She insisted he make love to her in Cantonese, *Gwongdung wah.* When he wanted to tease, he would speak Mandarin all evening, and she would laugh, holding her hands over her ears, saying *mouh yahn sik teng* — no one "knows how to hear," no one comprehends — and he would pull them away and whisper Northern endearments. After all these years, her Mandarin had become proficient; her ears were attuned to his accent. However, his *Gwongdung wah* never did sound quite right.

It wasn't a game anymore, hadn't been one for a long while.

"Will you drink with me?"

She considered a moment. "All right."

"Get us some glasses?" He began unwinding the wire on the cork.

She obliged, but noted the inexpensive brand, wondering, why couldn't he at least have brought Dom or something, if he must celebrate. She would have liked the treat, and it wasn't as if he couldn't afford it.

A quiet pop, unlike the shouting bullets of old. Before, she would let the froth and foam wash over her hands and lips, wetting her clothes, laughing as they fell upon each others' hearts. He still had beautiful hands, free of the welter of veins that plagued hers. Only the slightest tremor now as he poured.

"I'd have brought it over this morning. With a big bunch of pink roses and wild hybrids from Holland, and arranged them in your mother's vase before you got home, the way I used to surprise you."

She sipped rapidly at the overflow, in time to halt the spill. "At our age, we don't surprise."

He clinked her glass lightly before he drank.

In 1984, she had asked him to return the key to her flat.

"But why?" His shock was palpable.

"It would be more . . . convenient."

He had given her a sapphire and diamond bracelet that very evening, a gift for her forty-fifth birthday. What he didn't realize was that she knew it was originally a present for his wife who hadn't liked it because she wanted a certain Qing porcelain instead. He planned at first to return it to the jeweler, Linda Chow, but changed his mind at the shop. Her discovery of that fact had been entirely circumstantial. Linda Chow had wondered aloud about his decision to Jane Ho at their weekly *mahjeuk* table. Jane, being the incurable storyteller, repeated this when they'd run into each other one day, the way she'd probably told countless others, mindlessly, without real malice. Jane, of course, didn't know about them. Nobody did.

But that wasn't the reason she wanted her key.

"Convenient? For whom?" He almost shouted.

"Me of course. It is my home."

"I've never presumed otherwise."

"Then it isn't a problem?" She could not restrain the challenge in her voice.

He glared in cold anger, unyielding. "Tell me why."

"I think it's better if I don't, for both of us."

"I need to know," he insisted. And then, grazing her cheek with his fingers, "please?"

She refused to look at him. Since their life together began, she felt he adopted too Western a face, practically staring at people, and asking the same of her, insisting always that she "look at me." She complied out of consideration but found it alien. Right now, however, she looked away because she wanted to be honest. "It would be preferable to avoid unnecessary surprises."

When he left that afternoon, he did so in a fury, and refused to return for over a year. His absence saddened her a little, but did not cause heartache. She only wanted parity, but by then, she had lowered all expectations of him to virtually nil. It sufficed to embrace the memory of love. A pity, though, that she could never wear the bracelet publicly since Linda would be bound to recognize it, something that simply didn't occur to him. Discretion was her burden, not his.

Yet he did return, tortured by their time apart, unable to sever the connection. There isn't any reason to be angry, she reassured, as he undressed her, tore at her garments, drew her in greedily, desperately, reviving his soul.

He refilled his empty glass. "Do you still see . . .?"

She tried not to smile, but failed. He couldn't, had never

been able to ask the question outright, despite all his demands of others to be straightforward, railing against business associates, staff, friends, even family. His lack of diplomacy bled ink on the social pages.

"Not since the year before last."

"He was only the . . . second, right?"

"I believe in longevity."

Amusement lit his eyes, despite the jealous flash. He was youthful yet, and handsome; black strands lingered among the gray. He stood straight, conscious of his stoop. At nineteen, she had pledged passion to his image — hair like coal and eyes as warm as the sky on a summer's night. This afternoon he appeared tired; he allowed his shoulders to slump.

"I believed too, once."

Such maudlin tendencies! How she hated them. "You've had a good life."

"It's far from over. I still can, you know." He stretched an arm around her waist.

She pushed it way, exasperated. "Enough."

"Please."

"Don't make me pity you."

"I don't need pity. Just you."

"You don't need me. No one needs anyone."

His arm retreated and he sat down. "More champagne?"

She shook her head. When he had showed her the Viagara last year, gleefully, like a child, she almost lost her temper. That was when she told him not to visit again. He did, of course, because life could not keep them apart. "I'm tired," she declared.

"You don't eat enough." His voice rich with concern. "Let me order you some Hainan chicken rice. You like that. The broth will do you good."

Chicken rice again. Did he think she ate nothing else? "No. It'll spoil my appetite."

"Oh, are you going out tonight?"

"Why ask? You know I do every year."

"I'm sorry."

"Stop apologizing."

He took hold of both her hands. *"Qingfu,"* he said. Love-wife.

"Don't call me that. It's not what I am."

"I'm sorry."

And what she could recall of the night he first kissed her was that he said, afterwards, "I can't take you home."

She had been startled by the sensation of his proximity. Her whole body swayed dreamily, encouraged by the champagne. Everything about that almost midnight moment had been new, delicious, swaddling her legs, hips, waist, breasts, arms in a heavenly wrap. She hadn't quite heard what he said. "I'm sorry?"

"I can't take you home."

"Oh, that's all right." She supposed it was, because from the moment they met, a mere twenty minutes ago, reality disappeared, flushed away into nothingness.

"In fact, I have to find my partner. Before midnight."

She stared at him quizzically.

"I came with someone tonight. A woman."

She giggled. "Then you better not let her find us."

He scribbled her number in his notebook and promised to call. During the year that followed, she went often to meet him at cinemas, in parks, at bus stops. As long as her parents didn't know. They wouldn't have approved of this older man, this entrepreneur who rented out property for a living. Shameful, they would have called it. Exploiting your own kind. His later wealth and social standing would have justified nothing in their eyes.

All that year, he had begged her to surrender. Such nonsense, she'd say. You men make too much of all that. Then it shouldn't matter, he argued. Privately, she agreed, although she wouldn't say so to him. What she wanted was to know the certainty of her love. He persisted. She found she needed to see no one else. He would wait, he said, until forever.

There was a moment she finally knew.

It was summer. Her mother had been coughing, and she was making soup for her as prescribed by their herbalist. As she hovered over the bitter aroma, she heard the faint cough. It brought her back to the day when she was four, holding onto her mother's hand as they left their home in Guangzhou. "We'll stay with uncle until we find our own place," her mother said, between coughs. "Will I like it over there?" she wanted to know. "Oh yes, your father has set up a nice shop for his antiques. On Hollywood Road, imagine, what a name for a street! We'll have a good life, you'll see." "How long will we live in Hong Kong?" "As long as you want. Until . . ." her mother searched for words to make her laugh. "Until the next century. How would you like that?"

Later that day, after her mother had fallen asleep, she went out to meet him. He reached for the tip of her nose in greeting. "Where to, today?"

She grabbed hold of his hand, cool and comforting in its closeness, and kissed him below the ear. "Forever," she replied.

He gripped her so tightly she could scarcely breathe. "You've made me the happiest man in the world."

Two days later, he told her that Janet Ogilvy had accepted his marriage proposal, and that they could no longer meet. The following year, her mother died. Her mother was fifty two.

"So why did you want to meet?" It was almost five thirty. She had to get ready soon. Tonight was exceptional. She was going to dinner and the Philharmonic's concert with Linda Chow, whose children were all in Canada, and who was alone since her husband's death three years ago. They were both expected at Jane Ho's party for the millennium moment. Linda was the punctual type; besides, there was no explaining him, especially not now.

"You haven't drunk yours."

"I don't drink much anymore." She did not hide her impatience.

He swiveled his champagne flute on its base. "I have to go soon too."

Then stop wasting time, she wanted to say. Out with it. Instead she waited, thinking, he had become, not exactly annoying or boring, but something she didn't recognize.

"Janna's getting divorced. She called from London." He meant his third child, the daughter after Janet's first miscarriage.

"That's a shame. I hope she knows she can come home if she wants." Because Janna didn't get along with her mother.

"My children, they're all so . . . English."

She almost shouted — well what did you expect? Hadn't she warned him, urged him to be a father, to show his children his love. They can't read your heart, she'd told him over and over again. You have to show them you care by the things you do, not by what you say. He had been at home so little, and Janet was an Anglophile. It was useless repeating herself. Things were hard on all five kids since Janet floated off into her own "spiritual" space after the cancer. Yet as she looked into his troubled eyes, she failed to connect, failed to feel anything more than a polite sympathy. Neither he, nor anyone, deserved the sorrows of life.

Yet surely their paths forked and always had? Unlike her, he had no family and tried to create his own. Janet Ogilvy was beautiful once, and Eurasian, with privileged access into colonial English society. It was what he chose in marrying . . . no, it was more than mere choice. He desired, lusted after, craved all that Janet represented so desperately that it became something else, something stronger. A feeling like love.

"I don't have anyone to talk to," he complained.

"You have family, friends, your club, the world. You've been knighted by the queen and shaken hands with Deng. All of Hong Kong knows who you are."

"I need you."

"No you don't."

"You're still angry."

"No."

"Forgive me?"

"I am not angry at you. I've never really been angry."

"Then why won't you love me anymore?"

He had drunk too quickly and too much. She had to get him out before he made a fool of himself. Taking hold of his glass, she tried to wrest it gently away, expecting his fingers to loosen. He surprised her by gripping the stem.

"Don't patronize me."

She pulled up her hands as if he'd pointed a pistol at her. "Done."

"Marriage is the beginning of death," he told her when they met again, seven years after his wedding. She had not attended. Her presence would have upset Janet, who suspected, but did not know of their little affair. At twenty, she had had no great expectations after her virginal sacrifice. He had been fun, a break from life's routine, a passion tornado.

By now, he was rising in society and reasonably wealthy.

They had run into each other on Hillwood Road near her home. He was driving past when he spotted her.

"And what about you? Why haven't you married?"

"No one wants me," she smiled.

"Still the joker."

"Life isn't so serious."

"That's easy for you to say, with no family responsibilities."

She wanted to say, parenthood can be planned, but refrained. Her father taught that incivility did not become a lady. "So how many now?"

"Three. Another girl. Janet wants at least two more."

"How nice. Well, pleased to see you again. Give Janet my regards." Her father wasn't well and she wanted to get back to him.

But he dallied. "You're still very beautiful."

"We spinsters keep well."

"Can I come see you?"

"And 'be the number three'?"

He laughed. "Why not? It's quite 'expected,' as you Cantonese say."

Afterwards, she regretted it. She hadn't meant at all to suggest . . . she had no desire for an affair. No reason either to tell him about Joseph Chan, the civil servant who wanted to marry her and would have made a fine husband. She couldn't explain her reluctance. Love was deaf to mere declarations, and marriage, at least to Joseph, seemed unnecessary.

Perhaps if her father had lived, she would never have quit teaching or gone abroad for her Ph.D., and their lives could have progressed as friendly, if distant, acquaintances. She did not regret starting what they called their "silly people's secret thing" when they became lovers and continued during her time in the U.S. Wonderful memories, sweetened by age. He looked so tired now, so burdened by life. What did his ambitions matter anymore?

He poured himself more champagne and sipped, wistfully perturbed.

"What do you want from me?" she asked.

"I don't know."

"Things aren't the same."

"But why not? Why won't you tell me? We've been together so long you've become a part of me. Don't take that away. It's pointless to separate now. Let me see you. We belong to each other." His voice trembled. "Besides, you owe me, just a little don't you think?"

"I don't owe you. You told me yourself the very day we met." The day, she knew, he gave the gift of love, without expectations or demands.

"It isn't about that. I love you."

"Don't confuse yourself."

"Then what? Because you think I can't?"

She grimaced. "Don't be ridiculous. It was never just about sex."

"Then why won't you love me?" When she gazed at the ceiling and did not reply, he repeated, "it's because you think I can't, isn't it? Isn't it?"

Always, always. It would always be about him. She refused to break her gaze.

Thirty, she mused, had been her year to take a stand. It was the year she quit teaching and attended, reluctantly, a New Year's Eve party. He was there alone. Janet was ill.

That night, he took her home and made her feel nineteen again.

His visits were sporadic at first. Her father was already dead and she owned the family flat where she lived alone. He came more often; it became like his second home, but without his contribution. Had he offered money, pride would have insisted she refuse it.

She wanted more of him, but did not demand, knowing it wouldn't be fair. Two years later, she left for graduate school in Massachusetts. Away from home, their relationship became real.

He declared love a lot, and most of the time, she ignored him. He needed to brag; the rest of his life did not allow such space. After each visit he paid her abroad, he would report back greater successes, in business and social affairs. That's excellent, she'd tell him, now don't talk too long or your telephone bill will clear out your bank account. Olden days. Easy hours peering at art slides and researching her thesis. Days to dream about going home, to take over the modest business her father left behind. Daughter, we're proud of you, she could hear her parents say. Their voices softened her loss, making it possible to go on.

Only once did she believe his declaration.

It happened when May flowers bloomed. After four years, he was impatient for her return. "I hate leaving you," he said. "Why don't you come home?" He said that often now, which she usually dismissed with a joke. But this time, something stirred. Perhaps it was the darling buds. "Why should I hurry back? It's more awkward for us there." He kissed the tip of her nose. "We can change that." For a moment, life burst open in magnificent radiance, although she remained cautious. "What is it you intend to do?" That was when he declared, "I love you. I'll leave Janet."

For once, she was silent. A promise of life demanded real attention. "You're not serious."

"I am."

"Why?"

"She doesn't make me happy the way you can. She doesn't understand me."

"What would we do?"

"I'd buy us a new home and I'll begin again. It would have to be a bigger place than yours, so that my children can visit. I won't be cruel to Janet. I know you wouldn't want me to do that. Everything will be fair."

Forget!

"What's the matter?" He had come out of himself and the champagne. "You look upset."

"It's nothing. I haven't been well."

"You see, I knew it. You haven't been eating enough, have you?" He stood and gripped her shoulders. "You need me."

Dirty dishes and stained sheets marched past the years. Her friends marveled that she never kept a domestic helper. How could she, if she didn't want word to get out, if she didn't want people to know? No, it was impossible. People in America do their own housework so why shouldn't I? She faced their world, defiant.

On the table, a puddle of spilt champagne.

"Stop it," she said. "Leave me alone."

He attempted an embrace, pinning her firmly against him. "One more time, please?" He licked her neck.

How could she tell him she felt nothing, that she had stopped feeling years ago?

"I'm not angry at you anymore," he reassured her. "Not even about your young men, when you made a fool of yourself. It was some mid-life thing. Tougher for a woman. I've forgiven you."

She shoved him away. "You're the fool."

"*Gwongdung* dragon." His voice was teasing. "My only love."

"Leave, please. Or I'll tell Janet." It burst out, escaping her lips. The words whirled chains before his eyes. She had never threatened. Not once.

He gazed at her in silent horror. "After all this time? Why?"

Because, exploded the silent scream, because you were unfair. To me, to all your children, to Janet. You perpetuated what you had no business doing. You made a mockery of truth and a fool of me. You promised without the intent to fulfill and worse, expected forgiveness. Life isn't about forgiveness and the wasting of our energies. Life is about love, not just the feeling of love.

The silence gripped her. She was sixty and still she hadn't spoken.

"You don't mean it," he said.

"I do."

He froze. His whole body seemed to shrink. And then his eyes searched round the flat. She removed his jacket from the closet.

"Oh," he began.

She knew what would follow — you hung it up, how kind of you — uttered in obtuse surprise. His words would have unleashed the scream completely, and then there would be no going back. She spoke before he could. "I'll be your *qingfu.*"

The day she first said that was two years after her return

from the U.S. They had not seen each other in months, not since he admitted he could not leave Janet and his family, and begged to end their relationship.

"I shouldn't be here," he said when he arrived, his arms filled with roses.

The petals were too open, she thought, as she placed them in water. "What do you want from me?"

"I can't let you go."

"Why not? I did." Only lightness and air, no betrayal of hurt. When her mother was dying and she knew it, she hadn't been able to stop her tears. *Don't*, her mother told her. *Live for love, not pain. Only fools carry pain as if their hearts depend on it. Look after your father. That's all I ask.*

"It destroys me to think of you with someone else."

Joseph Chan had taken her to the last New Year's ball, and she knew he'd seen her. "That's ridiculous. You ended it."

He became curt. "We've been through all that."

"Then there's nothing more to say."

He reached for her waist. "I love you."

She held herself away from him. "I know that."

"But it wouldn't be fair to make you my . . ."

"What?" Her eyes glimmered with laughter and tears. "Your *qingfu?*"

"No! I wouldn't waste your life like that."

"It isn't yours to waste."

"What do you mean? Don't you want someone to look after you?"

That was the first moment her burden of shame lightened. If she kept him, the power would be hers. She had looked after her father and because of it the pain of his death hadn't cut as deep. If she cared for him too — he brought laughter, after all, and at least the feeling of love — her life might be a little less empty.

"*Qingfu.* It's just a word," she told him.

His eyes lit up with the exhilaration of success. "Then you don't mind? You'll take me back?"

Very well, she decided. There wasn't really anyone else she wanted. Had she become his wife, marriage might have been the beginning of death. But to be his *qingfu,* the "wife" who gives the feeling of love . . . even if she would never forgive him, she could at least forgive herself for indulging in sorrow over his betrayal, and absolve herself of that intense, unbearable, private shame, more painful because she couldn't shout it to the world. Their "silly people's secret thing." Like the secret of the king's donkey ears, the words floated away with the winds, freeing her.

"You will?" Hope returned to his eyes.

"In memory."

His face fell. "But we've been together . . . over forty years."

"My parents didn't even have that many," she replied. "Besides, it was really thirty. I count us only from after your marriage. Thirty good years, though."

"But what will you do?"

"It's not like I depend on anyone. I'll do what I've always done. Look after the store, travel, see people, celebrate each New Year's Eve because my friends throw the best parties. These days, I may even meet another Beijing man." She giggled like a nineteen year old.

He frowned. "But what will I do?"

You, she wanted to ask. Do you really think this is still about you? His voice betrayed such worry that she had to choke back her laughter.

"Well, I'm glad you're amused." He put on his jacket, miffed but resigned.

Kissing his cheek, she was struck by its papery texture. "You, my love," she whispered to the air, "are a freed man." The door closed behind him.

Six o'clock. Heavens, how late. She really must make a move. She needed to get ready for the night ahead, for the pleasures that were yet to come.

INSIGNIFICANT MOMENTS
IN THE HISTORY OF HONG KONG

*"It doesn't matter if a cat is black or white,
as long as it catches mice."* Deng Xiao Ping

Monday, June 30, 1997. Hong Kong, BCC. 1430 Hrs.

"*Wei*, you eaten yet?" Lam Yam Kuen greets his Uncle Cheuk.

The older man raises his eyebrows. "Ah Kuen, what're you doing here? Aren't you working today of all days?"

"Later. My shift starts at four." Yam Kuen looks around the nearly empty restaurant. "Hey, got anything left in your kitchen?"

The lunch hour rush is over. Cheuk, who owns this place near the escalator, points to the staff lunch table. "Come join us. What, don't they feed you at that fancy club?"

"Aah, you know how it is. Cooks who make too much *gwailo*-Chinese food lose their touch for the real thing." It's the kind of talk that amuses his uncle, and Yam Kuen likes to indulge him.

This morning, he woke up thinking of Uncle Cheuk. When he was growing up, he spent many holidays in the New Territories with his uncle. The first time they met, he stayed for several months, because his father had to go into China to bring his mother out. Uncle's house was in a village near Shatin. It was old and spacious, with a red-tiled roof and stone floor. On weekends, his uncle would invite friends over and cook up country-style feasts. He prepared everything in a huge wok that sat on an open brick stove. Uncle loved that home. But the house is gone now, as is the village, which has been replaced by a private, high-rise housing development.

They sit down to eat with the cook and waiters. One of the waiters fills each person's rice bowl, while another places dishes of hot food on the table. Salted fish and pork, shrimp scrambled in egg, and as the vegetable, water spinach, ideal for summer. Yam Kuen's mouth waters.

"So how's business?" he asks.

"Good right now. Lots of tourists and foreign journalists. We even ran out of English menus." In between mouthfuls of rice, Cheuk calls to the dishwasher standing in the back next to the kitchen door. "Siu Gau, you feed the cat?"

"Madame on mezzanine fed it too much again. You know how she is," Siu Gau replies. "That cat is one fat critter."

"And it's scared of mice! When it sees a mouse it runs the other way. You saw that, right?" Cheuk waves his chopsticks to illustrate its flight path.

Siu Gau ambles over and sits at a nearby table. He's a young guy who only recently started working for Cheuk. "Yeah, saw that. Crazy, black-and-white, flea-infested thing."

"Scared of mice. Some cat." Cheuk laughs heartily, a big belly laugh. His few remaining grey strands of hair frame an open face, a moon face of smiles.

"That's 'cos it's neither black nor white," Siu Gau adds. "Not like 'Honorable Sir' Deng's!"

Everyone, except Cheuk, laughs. Yam Kuen feels at home here. It's been awhile since he's visited. He really should come by more often. His mother keeps reminding him that his uncle is getting old and has no one, since he never married.

The restaurant is small; it seats around fifty and serves home-style dishes, mostly for a dinner crowd. Its specialty is snake, a winter delicacy. When his uncle first opened it several years ago, Yam Kuen would stop by all the time for a late meal and occasionally join the *mahjeuk* table. His mother complained, saying he should know better than to impose. But as long as business was good, Uncle didn't mind.

Yam Kuen glances across the room at the only foreign customer who is by himself. "Think the *gwailo's* a journalist?"

Siu Gau doesn't glance at the man. "Not likely. Journalists, like policemen, get free meals. Food for words." He addresses Cheuk. "Isn't that right, boss?"

"They're just doing their job, that's all," Cheuk replies.

"Well, you know how it is. If Yung Kee gets a write up, it's because they've fed the right people." Siu Gau refers to the famous roast goose place nearby to the east of them, in the heart of Central business district. It's been written up countless times in the local and foreign press. "Our goose is the same, but cheaper!"

"You talk too much, you know that? Go feed the cat," says Cheuk.

Siu Gau strolls out the door.

His uncle doesn't like the dishwasher, Yam Kuen thinks. He doesn't know why; the kid's just young, and seems harmless enough. "So, are you going to see the fireworks tonight?"

Cheuk shrugs. "Are you?"

"I'll watch them on the big screen at work. It's supposed to be a super event, although tomorrow night's the real extravaganza. Eight million they're spending. Mainland money, you know." He wishes he could bring his uncle to the club, to watch the homecoming with him.

"Fireworks, hah. If you see one, you've seen them all. Doesn't matter who foots the bill." Cheuk lays down his chopsticks. He gulps tea, swishing the liquid around his mouth before he swallows. "Tonight, I'm 'opening a table.'"

Yam Kuen smiles at the familiar declaration. Uncle Cheuk, he decides, will continue playing *mahjeuk* right up to his deathbed.

Tuesday, July 1, 1997. Hong Kong, SAR. 1830 Hrs.

At Butterfield's Soong Club in Tai Koo Place, *maitre d'* Lam Yam Kuen ushers the first guests to arrive for Mr. Victor

Chacko's party of ten. The Keralan columnist is a regular patron. "He's a famous and well respected journalist," he tells his staff, even though Lam hasn't read Chacko's columns because they're limited to the English language press.

The first guests: a thin Caucasian woman and her Chinese husband. The latter speaks rather too loudly in American accented English. Probably an ABC, Lam thinks.

A rookie waiter offers the couple. "May we serve you your welcome cocktail?"

"What's in it?" The man asks. "Is it alcoholic?" His wife wants to know.

Lam jumps in, seeing the bewilderment on his staff's face. "It's grenadine, seven-up and vodka, but we can serve it without alcohol if you prefer." These days, it's difficult getting decent help, and the staff sometimes try his patience. Lam is fed up of rescuing rookies, but what choice does he have? He has to do his job.

"So what do you think, honey?"

Before the husband can answer, a cacophonous squeal fills the entrance and in roll the three Chacko children with their father, followed by their English mum. Adopted children, two Chinese girls and a Korean boy who speak perfect British English.

Mrs. Chacko greets Lam. She is always gracious, never condescending, unlike some of the English women he's had to serve over the years at other private clubs in Hong Kong. She is almost as tall as he is, and, at five eleven, he is a tall Chinese.

"Oh, Lam," she says, "my children are misbehaving again." She welcomes her guests. Into this midst races a Eurasian girl child, who has detached herself from her European father, behind whom follows the tenth and last guest, a stout Chinese woman in a long skirt who looks like a university professor. Lam knows Chacko's tables are never like anyone else's. He imagines Uncle Cheuk's face were he to see all this, and the funny, disbelieving grin that would erupt.

The restaurant fills up. Lam expects a full house. Fortunately, no one called in sick. A family crowd tonight, all the thirty and forty-something Chinese members. No one likes to cook on a public holiday.

Buffet night. Diners begin scoping out the adjoining room where the spread is laid out. Earlier, Lam inspected it, approving the arrangement. At the appetizer section, Cantonese roast goose and suckling pig, boiled chicken and barbecued pork, a cold platter of jellyfish, vegetarian "meats" and an array of sauces — ginger and garlic, plum, oyster, soy, spicy chilli. Next to these are the Western salads, lettuces and leaves never seen in the outdoor markets. Chicory, romaine, arugula, endive, mache, basil, accompanied by cold cut platters, as good as any five-star hotel buffet. All this, even before the prime rib and cornucopia of hot dishes comprising nearly every edible four-legged, winged and aquatic creature in an international variety of preparations — Indian and Malay curries, Thai spices, Indonesian satays — on the side, Buddhist broccoli.

Yet all the children want, once they've devoured what their parents decree, is vanilla or chocolate ice cream covered in sticky, sweet, multi-colored sauces.

When the giant screen lights up, all heads turn towards the

image of a translucent Pearl-of-the-Orient helium bubble floating across the harbor. Except at the Chacko table, where children giggle, the room is silent. Lam watches the other floats go by as he patrols the dining room.

At one table, a mother calls her son to her side, insisting he see the leaping white neon rabbit as it sails across the screen. *A white rabbit lives on the moon,* she says, *every child knows that.* Her son watches obediently, fixated.

The first night Yam Kuen stayed at Uncle Cheuk's place, he was six. A full moon illuminated the clear sky. Uncle took him for a walk in the fields. He had been a little scared and confused, unsure of this man, his mother's older brother, whom his father had brought him to meet.

"Do you remember your mother, Ah Kuen?" his uncle asked.

Yam Kuen shook his head. He hadn't seen her since he was two.

"My sister's tough, and patient. She wasn't afraid to wait alone on the Mainland because that was the only way."

Yam Kuen didn't know what to say. They walked awhile in silence. And then, Uncle stopped and pointed at the moon. "Can you see the rabbit up there? You can see him more clearly out here in the country."

Yam Kuen glanced up uncertainly. "Where?"

"In the right corner. He's receiving guests at home tonight. Squint hard."

He squinted and tried to make out the shape. Nothing. His uncle didn't say a word. He turned his head this way and that, searching as he squinted. Where was that rabbit? He looked at his uncle, who waved towards the night sky, gesturing for him to concentrate. "Be patient, Ah Kuen." Just when he was about to give up in frustration, the rabbit miraculously appeared, a dark outline against the light. "There it is, there it is!"

Uncle Cheuk laughed his big belly laugh, and rubbed Yam Kuen's head. "See how easy that was? You wait, when your mother comes home it'll be just as easy as seeing the rabbit. Don't you worry."

The fireworks begin. Cantonese television commentary fills the room.

Fifteen minutes into the program, the Chacko table disperses. Lam bids them goodbye, and ensures that one of his assistants sees them to the door. They head out towards the bullet elevators, discussing taxi arrangements.

Lam continues watching the show. What a shame those children won't get to see the full spectacle of tonight's fireworks and the finale. He hopes his uncle isn't missing it, because even at this early stage, tonight's display is already so much greater and grander than that of the night before.

BLACKJACK

In Trump's Casino, Atlantic City, I wander past the roulette table. Red or black, odd or even. I've never liked playing the numbers. One in thirty six aren't my kind of odds.

But blackjack! My kind of game. Stay, hit. Ten and six are sixteen. Hit me. Busted by an eight. An even handed tension.

I'm finally going home, going back to Hong Kong.

The rhythm at the table energizes and soothes. A six and seven, broken by a ten. Two kings, split bet. Next hand. Five cards total eighteen. I play for hours, winning, losing, winning again, losing again. Playing the dealer, playing the house.

No one expects to beat the house. No one.

"Why did you come back?"

The woman who questions me over dinner at the Cleveland Restaurant is a New Yorker, married to a Hong Kong Chinese. They've been "back" two years.

"My parents are old. I'm their only daughter."

"So bring them to the States. Aren't they nervous about '97?" And then, more to herself than to me, "isn't everyone?"

I'm glad dinner is almost over. It was a mistake looking up these friends of friends — all he can talk about is Shenzhen property, in which he's determined to make his fortune to bring back to America; she talks at me with that "why did I ever come to Hong Kong" glare. Dinner's been interrupted three times by calls to his portable phone.

We say our goodbyes, make polite noises about staying in touch. Do they guess how little I want to see them again? As I head towards the Causeway Bay MTR stop, I think no, they can't possibly know, because they haven't paused to reflect, because they don't know how to look inward for happiness.

Sixteen years ago, I left Hong Kong because I fell in love. He would never live anywhere but Brooklyn.

On a chilly, midsummer night eight years ago on a Long Island beach, I walked for hours, the divorce from my American husband still a fresh, stinging pain. *Geuitauh mohng mihng yuht* — the siren poem of every *wah kiu* — how easily moonlight invoked my city-village.

Yet New York city engulfed me for another eight years. My parents visited, and exclaimed *aiyah!* we could never live here among these dangerous black and brown *gwais!* and fled back each time to the safety of the known. So much for my precious U.S. passport and democratic embrace of multicultural life. In the meantime, the eighties spun out of control on Wall Street. A year after Black Monday, the investment bank for which I worked handed out pink slips to four hundred employees, me included.

What ever happened to that lucky Chinese eight?

By the nineties I said enough, *gau, gau lah.*

So I came back, two months ago, and found a job as everyone said I would. A good job, with a large office and a secretary, well paid, at more than my last U.S. salary. I even like my work, because my colleagues treat me seriously, just as they treat their own positions seriously.

I'm beginning to believe in the future again.

Now here I am at midsummer, gambling on five years on, with my own kind.

The MTR is a vast echo chamber. I like it at night, when no one does the hundred yard dash into position between the painted lines. It's almost midnight, but I'm not afraid. Back in New York, I did the daily Manhattan transfer only by day, only when I had to, and even then, the stations reeked of their nocturnal function.

Three stops — "left and right of ten minutes" spins the Cantonese in my head — and I'm back in Tsimshatsui. Before I left the States, I learned to stop including Tsimshatsui in my forwarding address because no one could pronounce it, let alone handle the spelling. Do you dream in color or black and white? Cantonese or English? In New York subway cars, desperate southern Chinese immigrants seek me out to point them towards Chinatown. They are not my people, not Hong Kong *yan,* because they haven't been infected by our linguistic schizophrenia.

I dream in psychedelic Chinglish, with bits of Putonghua

hovering, in preparation for my future masters.

"So what's going to happen in 1997?"

In New York, my friends were well informed. All the news that's fit to print has told them, in many more column inches than even five years ago, that Hong Kong and China are the must-know, must-read latest addition to their information overload.

I came home because I was tired of telling people that nothing or everything was going to happen in 1997.

"But aren't you afraid?"

Along the walls of the escalators in the MTR, a blast of color persuades, induces, entices and coerces me to buy, buy, buy. Our leaders are not on television telling us to go out and spend a little. Our leaders are not in concert denying a layoff-ridden recession. Hong Kong *yan* are not afraid to work, work, work in order to buy, buy, buy, after which they let their spirits soar to the strains of karaoke.

Why should I be afraid?

I came home because I was tired of being afraid of another possible layoff and the shrinking unemployment fund.

How bad can it be? Nero was probably laughing to the strains of his violin.

I exit to the streets of Tsimshatsui into the cool aftermath of yesterday's typhoon. It is surprisingly quiet. I search the avenues of my memory, of a remembered Tsimshatsui of my childhood. Where are the "Blitish" soldiers and Yankee sailors prowling along Canton or Mody Road? Where are the orange-haired teenage prostitutes roosting outside Chungking Mansion? Now, everything is sleek and shiny, a never ending mirror of modernity.

Even the streets are cleaner than I remember.

I feel the onset of insomnia. Guaranteed, Mother will be up — the rhythms of our bodies have always moved in time, even across the globe — and she will work the conversation around to her favourite topic, my marital prospects. I've already heard about Mrs. Chan's "boy," the forty-five year old never-been-married bachelor who is liberal about divorce, making good money as an account director at a 4A agency. And then there's the Yih "boy," divorced with one child to support (but only one girl, no trouble, girls) who wants to get married again. You can tell she's desperate because she even endorses my secondary school boyfriend James Choy, The Eurasian (a doctor, not so bad in the end! and after a *gwailo,* a Eurasian is acceptable, even desirable) who was widowed last year.

Instead of going home, I head to the Peace Cafe to listen to Cole Porter and Jerome Kern *et al.*

It's emptying out, which is the way I like it. Why does everyone call Hong Kong overcrowded? Perhaps I have a knack for finding the empty spaces, the aces in the hole, when necessary.

Multinational city. Australians singing American jazz. Chinese and Western audience listening and not listening. A make-believe world deliberately reminiscent of Shanghai.

My father fled Shanghai in 1949.

My mother tried to flee Hong Kong in 1969.

In 1979, I pledged allegiance to a distant flag, all because I had fallen for my man and his "friendly green card acquisition with strings attached."

Flee, fly, mosquito. I returned to hear the Girl Guide song I used to sing around campfires in the New Territories, you know, the once upon a fast disappearing countryside?

I've got you, under my skin. I've got you, deep in the heart of me. The singer croons. Slick jazz, doesn't dare improvise. Shimmering on the surface of this highly polished pearl.

In the Village Vanguard in between McCoy Tyner's sets, I tried to answer my friend's question. No, I said, I am not afraid of 1997.

One day, a red flag will fly over Hong Kong.

Carpe diem. Mao believed in seizing the day. So did Robin Williams. There. It's that forked voice again. Dead poets have many tongues.

In my girl guide company way back when, one girlfriend would never stand for "God Save the Queen" claiming she was Chinese, not British. Yet she wore the blue uniform proudly, and even made Queen's guide. Later, she went to England to study and acquired a posh accent. Now, she stakes her and her children's future on Hong Kong, post 1997.

About a week before I finally left the States, I made my trip to Atlantic City.

Around the slot machines, senior citizens rooted, discarding nickels, dimes and quarters. I watched one lady win $700 in the quarter machine, only to lose it all within half an hour. She was happy though. This was her retirement pleasure, her earned peace.

Hong Kong's changed a lot, are you sure you want to come back? Even my parents, pleased by this uncharacteristic Confucian filial bent, cautioned before my return.

You're an American now, you even watch baseball. My American friends, well meaning, cannot fully accept this decision.

Blackjack. Black hair. Black eyes.

Sixteen years . . .

No time to feel, no time to ponder. Split second decisions.

Five years on . . .

Twenty one!

Sometimes you win, sometimes you lose. Next hand.

THE EIGHTIES

MANKY'S TALE
for Malcolm Brashear

My sister So-kit appears, out of nowhere, and declares. "I marched." She is crying.

I'm listening to the tape Skip Yam gave me last week. He's a musician and sound man who records local jazz bands. The mix of pipa and saxophone is curious.

So-kit demands. *"Wei,* take your headphones off a minute and listen. I marched."

The phone rings. It's my wife, Rosa-M, calling from Springfield, Masschusetts. "Hold on a sec," I tell her. "What are you talking about?"

My sister shivers through her tears. "Tiananmen," she says and leaves.

Over the phone, Rosa-M says. "Manky, everyone's talking about what's happening in Beijing. I'm frightened."

I turn on the TV. The local news is full of the evening's marchers, a long snake of people weaving through the streets of Hong Kong. "Same here."

"When are you coming home?"

"Come on, honey, we've been through that. My father's really ill." She starts to cry. All the women in my life are drowning in tears. "Please don't, Rosa-M."

"Please come home," she begs.

"As soon as I can."

There are times I wish Rosa-M were not my wife. She needs so much — attention, worry, care, even sex. She needs money, to live with sufficient passion and frivolity. Most of all, she needs family, meaning me, because she abhors her own and does not know the bonds of a real family.

How different it was when we met! Then, she became *my* real family because I played jazz.

Every afternoon, I hear my mother's voice tremble before we go visit Dad at Queen Mary. The cancer is inoperable. We stare at him, helpless, waiting without hope, as we've done for weeks. *Any time.*

Today he sends my mother away. "Let me speak to our son alone." Reluctantly, she steps out of his room.

"A-Jaai," he begins, and struggles to sit up.

"A-Ba." I reply.

"It's bad."

"I know."

He tries to drink some water and I help. Only two weeks ago, he appeared strong, almost healthy. I could picture him getting dressed in his suit, preparing for work, knotting his tie into a perfect double knot. The deftness with which he always did that amazed me, the way he was as long as I can remember. A perfect civil servant.

"My retirement money. Did you move it into your mother's account?"

"Yes."

"Close the joint account. Less troublesome for the probate."

My heart cracks. "Don't . . ."

He signals for me to be quiet. "It's okay. These things must be done, but I don't like to upset your mother."

I sit by his bed, wanting to touch his hands, his face, any part of him. I don't. My father and I do not touch.

He says. "Your sisters still aren't married."

"They're young."

"So-kit's over thirty, and So-si turns thirty this year. What's wrong with girls today?"

His frown makes me smile. "They don't need men these days."

"Your wife does."

I hold my tongue. There was a time the bite in his words would make me mad, and I'd argue back. He doesn't think much of Rosa-M because she isn't nice to my mother. It's not entirely Rosa-M's fault, although I do wish she'd try a little harder. They come from such different universes; even my sisters don't get along great with her. So-si's nicer, but then, she's sweet to everyone.

The night Rosemary Hui walked into the Arts Center way back when, I hardly noticed her. She wasn't my "Rosa-M" yet. Some South African chap, a Shakespeare professor from Hong

Kong U, occupied her space. I was trying to get a drink along with the other band members. The last set wore me out. It was hot and smoky. That top floor lounge wasn't really designed for music, but hey, it was a jazz gig, and those were hard to come by then. I was the only local drummer who would play with the "ghost people," and Tim Wesson, the band leader, an American who'd been in Hong Kong, forever it seemed, was a friend.

Rosemary didn't pay me no mind. I thought she was one of those girls with a taste for foreign men. Didn't seem at all interested in me. Don't even know how we wound up talking. All I know is I ended up with her number and the rest is history as we know it.

Yet to hear her tell! "He picked me up, and then chased me for weeks until I'd go out with him. Of course, he did rescue me from that *haahmsap lo,* my professor who thought he was such a Romeo. Falstaff, more like." All our friends laugh at her stories and love the tale of our romance. Our glorious romance, despite its inauspicious beginnings. "You met in a bar? In Hong Kong?" And I used to have to explain to our Chinese friends that it wasn't exactly a bar, that on alternate Saturdays, it became a space for jazz. Even in the late seventies, people here thought I was from another planet. No one listened to, let alone played, jazz.

Here. These days, I hardly dare call Hong Kong home. Whisper the slightest murmur and Rosa-M's off on a rampage. *America's our home now,* she insists. *Why do you hang onto all that past? I'm your family, your life, your home. Isn't that what marriage is supposed to be about?*

Anyone would think she were American born. No, I'm being unfair. She is *wah kiu* after all, a Chinese from Malaysia like her mother. This isn't home for her even though here was where she mostly grew up. Is it *my* fault her mother left her dad, took her away from Hong Kong, and then died on her before she turned ten? I'm sure it was hard. Her father's not a bad guy, but what am I supposed to do if they don't talk? You can't blame him for being lonely. It's been years since Rosa-M's mother died, and marrying a young woman from China isn't the worst thing for an old man.

I *got* us our J-1's, I'll *get* us our green cards, even if it means hanging up my sticks for now. How much more does she want? I'm as faithful and loyal as a husband should be. I've given body and soul.

What *else* must I give? The blood of my heart?

My father coughs. "Why won't you come home?"

"A-Ba, we've been through all that."

He looks as if he's about to say more, but stops. Then. "Lots of Chinese in Massachusetts?"

"What?" I am distracted by a news report from this radio he won't switch off. "Yeah, sure."

"Good Chinese?"

"What do you mean?"

"Can your sisters find husbands there?"

I laugh. My father's never been to America, has never had any desire to go. "A-Ba, do you think it's still the railroad days?"

"What railroad?" He sounds annoyed. "I'm serious. Plenty

of good schools in Boston, that's in Massachusetts, right? Medical schools. Business schools. Your sisters can find good husbands."

I try to imagine the conversation. *So-kit, So-si, as your honorable big brother, it is my responsibility to arrange marriages for you. Father has decreed.*

Right. They'd both tell me to take a flying leap.

Instead, I say. "What makes you think they'd leave A-Ma or Hong Kong? This is their home."

"So why aren't you with them?"

Always, it always comes back to this.

Last night's call went on for over half an hour. Cried me a river. Can't stand it without me.

"Don't leave me," she said when Dad first got ill, as if coming to see my family meant abandoning her. Didn't mean to lose my cool, but she was way out of line. Hey, my father's dying. What kind of son does she think I am? "You don't really love your family," she declared. "I've never even seen you hug any of them." That did it. *What the hell do you know about love*, I shouted, and we fought. Shattering. Like snares rattling round in my brain.

Oh, we made up. We generally do, though sometimes I want to get in the car and drive away forever. South. I'd head south and stop when I reached New York. Bring my sticks. Play again. Never look at another monitor full of code and databases.

But no. Couldn't do that to poor Rosemary.

Since I left with her for grad school six years ago, this is my first trip back. *Don't blame me,* she says. It's not like I do. We have our visas to think about; it's tricky making sure you don't jeopardize the green card. There's also her PhD to finish. Besides, we're broke and I haven't been at my job all that long. My boss was great about this though, told me to take all the time off I needed. He was awed by the distance, realizing I couldn't zip here and back as if it were, say, Boston.

Last night, there were moments I almost could leave her forever.

The nurse comes in with his medication. He thanks her, using that formal tone he reserves for everyone except family. I went to his office on Queensway once, three years before he retired, and remember the way he addressed his secretary. *Miss Chan* — he almost bowed — *I introduce you to my son who plays drums and computers,* and the poor woman had to fight to suppress her giggles. It was before I brought Rosa-M home, back in the day when he liked to find me nice girls.

My mother sticks her head in. "I have to cook dinner."

I get up and go to her.

"You go," he says. "I want Man-kit to stay."

They nod to each other and she departs. I go back to his bedside and stand there.

He declares. "I will miss her."

"Come on, A-Ba."

He reaches out and his fingers graze my hand. "It's all right."

I cannot sit and walk by the window. The news announcer continues to invade this space.

He speaks to my back. "Bad time to be any kind of

Chinese." His breath is labored.

"What can we do about blood?"

"They said a million people."

I turn to face him. "So-kit marched, you know."

He looks surprised, shakes his head and smiles. "Well. So some thoughts *do* occur, even at the hairdresser's."

We both laugh.

For as long as I can remember, my mother has never washed her own hair. She goes, once a week, religiously, to the same man in Causeway Bay she's gone to for years. When So-kit started work after secretarial school, she got into the same habit, although she had to find her own, more fashionable man, one who doesn't pretend to be straight. Only So-si has had the presence of mind to shuck off this frivolous habit, although even she finds washing her own hair a pain.

Before I left for the States, I told Dad that the women in our family would never leave home because their hairdressers won't let them.

"Your aunt," he says.

He means his only sister, who's five years older and in a home. She never married. "I'll take care of her, I promise."

"Bring your mother to visit. Your A-Ma doesn't like going alone, and So-si works far too much."

My youngest sister is in film production and her hours are crazy. Between Dad and me, it goes without saying that So-kit, who does have time, will never adopt the caretaker role. "I will."

"When are you leaving home?"

I want to reply, I'll be *going home*. Instead. "In due course."

He leans his whole body back, and his head slips down onto the pillow. His eyes waver. It's the medication. Makes him tired.

I say. "Tomorrow, then?"

He nods. Before he slips into sleep, he whispers. "Take them away, all of them. Your U.S. citizenship. Get it."

I am startled. My father never wanted another passport for our family.

I can't speak to Rosa-M tonight. So-kit can tell her I'm sleeping. I'm going out, but I'd rather she not know. She gets jealous, unnecessarily, even while telling me about some former student who's lusting after her. Some joker with a pet snake. Her logic's absurd.

Tim and Skip are playing The Jazz Club. Wish this place had been around before. Some American cat's on bass, Charlie Mason, a friend of Tim's who also used to be with the Philharmonic. First time hearing him and I like what I hear. They ask me to sit in. I tell Skip I haven't played in over a year. He says it's time I got some practice.

Rosa-M would like this club.

There was a time we lived in clubs. When we first got to America, it was all we did. See, she used to say, *here's* the home of jazz. If you really want to understand the heart of something, you've got to taste its roots and live its history. We went everywhere in our beat up VW bug. She bitched about the car, but hell, it ran.

We heard as much of the real thing as we could, live.

Opened my ears.

When did things change? Now, all I hear is the whine in her voice and I'm afraid that love too will become inaudible.

Now, I'm almost too scared to play anymore.

Elvin Jones. The time I saw him at the Vanguard, it was spiritual. His eyes were closed and his cymbals shivered through me. He rolled a rounded rhythm, smooth with energy, powerful, warm. We sat right up front, so close to the stage I could touch him.

That was when I first arrived in America, angry at my father who didn't, no, couldn't understand this "crazy-foreign jazz life" or my marriage. Listening to Elvin, I wanted to cry. He was playing to me, teaching me a lesson. He hit the crash cymbal so hard it flew off the bandstand. Barely missed my head by a centimeter. The audience gasped. Luckily, Rosa-M pulled me away towards her just in time. When he opened his eyes, he saw the fallen cymbal but never missed a beat.

Fear's a funny thing. It gets you if you let it.

Tonight, my father dies at ten minutes past eleven.

Tonight, the moment my sticks hit the drums, it was like I never left.

THE FOURTH COPY
or
DANCING WITH SKELETONS
AND OTHER ROMANCES

Let's start with Once Upon A Time.

One Of Those Perfect Sun Days, A Novel by Grace Hsu. Return address: Public Publishing Co., Parsippany, N.J.

The manuscript arrives in the mail to her Manhattan apartment. Grace Hsu flips through the pages of her first and only finished creative writing effort from a college course ten years ago. No marks, no cover letter. Just coffee stains on the first page.

Edvard Munch's "melancholy adolescence" — the subject of her current reading — snickers in the background.

By late afternoon, Grace Hsu, thirty, successful Communications Consultant to the Architectural Profession, immigrant of two years to New York, is seeking consultation from her favorite cousin, the architect.

"But Andy, who sent it? No one, other than my parents and the university library, has a copy. It was a thesis. I never tried to publish it."

Andy Djeng, long accustomed to the crazy life of his Hong Kong cousin, says, "What about your professor?"

"He died a year after I graduated."

"So check out the publishing company," he says.

Three days later, she calls him again.

"If Public Publishing Co. exists, or ever existed, it's managed to escape the notice of the telephone company, the Chamber of Commerce, the local bookstores, newspapers, and magazines. In fact, it's a phantom as far as the entire town of Parsippany is concerned. On top of that, the library copy hasn't been moved, and my parents have nothing to do with this. *Gwai gu.*"

"What was that?"

"Ghost story, in Cantonese."

"Is that what your novel is?"

"What?"

"A ghost story."

"You know, I don't really remember."

"So why don't you read it. It'll take your mind off all this."

"But Andy . . . "

"So what's it about?"

"What?"

"Your novel, silly."

"Oh, it was, I don't know, about 'sun days.' Perfection, I guess."

"A notion long laid to rest in your life, right? Hey, we've got a presentation brochure to finish."

She hears him chuckle as he hangs up.

*

The opening paragraph of her manuscript reads:

"It was one of the those perfect sun days. Trees were just the right green, sky the right blue. Roads clean after last night's typhoon. Lazy sun day, nothing to do. Harbor still quiet in the early morning light. Rare day for her city.

"In this early morning, it was her city. No tangled traffic, nor blaring horns, nor screaming televisions. She was glad it was after the rains. None of that dog shit marred the beauty of her pavements. She loved walking in her city the way it was now. Pavements clean, the bowling alley still free from its habitual rumblings. Nothing open for business yet."

*

Grace wonders at this opening. Could five-million-people-in-less-than Manhattan-size Hong Kong once really have been her image for perfection?

The phone rings, and it's her sister in Paris. Part of Juliana's marketing research job involves making numerous international phone calls to never-to-be audited phone numbers. Juliana calls this and other trans-Atlantic calls her "executive perks," something she believes is more than owed her after the MBA — *summa cum laude* — and Parisian sexism when she job hunted.

Grace tells her the *gwai gu*.

Juliana says, "That was the story about your fear of dogs."

"Hey, you're right. I'd forgotten."

"How could you do that, forget I mean. After all, it's not as if you've written fifty novels."

"No, but . . ."

"You were going to become a writer."

Such accusation. Grace — tough enough to brazen divorce in Hong Kong, and then hightailing it back, alone, to the Land of Liberty — Grace has let her less tough, married-with-child, stuck-in-Paris Juliana down.

After the phone call Grace muses. A very long time since dogs were her adversary, or the eating of dog meat, or blood.

*

Her professor's voice infiltrates:

"The first time I saw you in class, a tiny Chinese girl, new in America, hair in pigtails, and you said you wanted to write about being scared of dogs, I didn't have much hope for your story. And then, this."

Grace awakes with a start. Three in the morning, glasses askew on her face, and the lights blazing in her living room. A fallen pillow and backache the only testimonials to her haphazard sleeping patterns.

The book on Munch lies open at a drypoint titled "Death and the Maiden, 1894." A naked young girl, her long black hair loose down her back, embraces a skeleton.

Round about the third draft, her professor had insisted, "But who's this 'Jimmy' in your story? You never make it quite clear."

She hesitated before replying, "Jimmy's the nickname her school gave the Biology lab skeleton."

"Then say so."

And she remembers the immense feeling of relief that overcame her: it was all right for a virgin to make love to a skeleton! Most of all, it was all right that she could have imagined it, could have conceived of it inside her secondary school life, and articulate it here in the Land of Liberty.

She glances again at the Munch. In any event, Munch thought it was all right too.

At the end of her novel, she is surprised to find a one page synopsis on the last page. It reads:

"It was one of those perfect sun days, no more no less. The sun reflected that very perfection in the park below. But she knew that perfection would have to be marred by the imperfect happenings of the day. Somehow, she never could retain those perfect moments. For an instance, she completely understood the feelings of Anny in Sartre's *Nausea*.

"If it were the wedding that bothered her, she showed no signs. The barkings in the distance drummed through her brain: one of these days, one of these perfect sun days . . .

"He could not have been happier. He had waited for this day for years. Years of longing, an unsatisfied craving. One day. For him it was today, wedding day.

"She raised the knife. It came down like a flash on the chopping block. The rawness of meat, the bloody mess that lay before her. The sun continued shining in the perfection of its day. Still time to retain perfection.

"She hid the knife under her pillow. Another victim of the block, another one to the slaughter.

"It was one of those perfect sun days, no more no less. The sun reflected that very perfection in her untouched self. Outside, the sirens screamed.

"He had only wanted a wife.

"The asylum at Castle Peak is quiet these days. There have been no outbursts lately. Just the occasional ones from the girl whose father sold dog meat."

*

Emerging from the West Fourth subway stop in the Village, she hears a man call, "Grace! Grace Hsu!"

A vaguely familar figure hurries through the crowds.

"My God, it is you. You haven't changed, Grace, not a bit. You could still be eighteen!"

Who is he, this rather stocky, curly haired man with a European accent? She smiles politely.

"You don't remember me?"

When it finally clicks that this is Vincent, that this is the college senior to whom she surrendered that precious virginity, she wants to laugh.

They go for a drink. He tells her all about his marriage and children and divorce. By the second drink, his voice is soft and warm and sentimental.

and all she can remember is that there was no blood, no pain, no feeling. just a horrible numbness, a sense of nothingness. that she had surrendered nothing, gained nothing. that a whole American freshmen year where students didn't study but worried about beer blasts and "scoring" was nothing, nothing, nothing she could ever explain to anything she came from. and a year later, that story that novel about perfection and blood as if the blood of her fictional murder could bring life into the madness of reality.

and all she can remember is that in hong kong, this place she

called home, everything submerged way down deep because there
was no space to say she was turned on by a boy who was ugly and
cerebral and not her own kind, that even now after the orgasms
her body responds to a cerebral stimuli before anything else.

and all she can remember is that she left something behind in
that novel, her copy, the fourth copy because

*

Let's begin again. It is one of those perfect sun days. Grace
Hsu sips her wine and smiles at the man to whom she gave up
her virginity ten years ago. He is a stranger now, who talks of
a life in America she never shared. All the time he speaks, her
mind returns to the novel. She remembers the scene with the
skeleton, when she finally called Jimmy the skeleton. The
protagonist, a Chinese girl at a Catholic school, is engaged to
a European boy who loves dogs. The boy wants to make love
to her, but insists that they wait because that would be proper.
The protagonist expresses no feelings about her virginity.

But in biology class, she is seduced by the skeleton. The
American nun who teaches biology is enthusiastic about her
subject, and names the skeleton. One night, at midnight of
course, the protagonist goes to the school for a rendezvous
with the skeleton. They dance, they embrace, they make love.
She has her first orgasm.

She is sixteen.

The man whom she loved at eighteen, and to whom she
gave up her virginity, recalls her to the present tense.

"Will I see you again, Grace? This is such a coincidence, and
surely, old friends should keep in touch? You look lovely."

This is not the way she remembers their original encounter

ten years ago. Then, he called her a baby freshman, who was not nearly as glamorous as the buxom blondes he was accustomed to dating. She remembers thinking that there was no such thing as a buxom blond Chinese. Of course, there were so few Chinese at her upstate alma mater: perhaps fifty in all, of which five were female. But that was normal, was reality.

So she says, "No, I don't think it would be a good idea. I'm seeing someone now."

"I understand," he says, smiling, friendly.

Does he suspect the lie, she wonders, as she watches him walk away.

*

But why kill him? Grace tosses this question around and around as she orders the events of her days. Telephone rings, messenger arrives, people people people in some form or other touching her life. And all the time, Grace wonders, why did she have to kill him?

For dramatic effect?

This is how she explained the story to friends in college:

"With the murder, she destroys the ugly side of life. Then, she isn't afraid of dogs any longer. At the asylum, she's surrounded by dogs, and perfect sun days."

A friend had said. "Sounds too unreal."

And she replied. "But who decides what reality is anyway?"

He dies, Grace thinks, because he is drunk. Yes, the lover cum husband is drunk on his wedding night, turning the first intercourse into a travesty. That's why he had to die. Narrative license, poetic convenience.

But.

There, Grace thinks, is that voice again. Where's it coming from? Telephone rings. Have to make another call. The prints won't be ready till Friday?! Why not?

But. The husband was drunk only in the story. The husband doesn't die in the novel. The one page synopsis was for the story, before it became a novel. Remember?

She doesn't remember as she calls cousin Andy to explain that she'll be ready for his presentation on Monday.

The original brochure reads:

"Architecture is both an art and a science. The architect must blend the structural integrity of design with the demands imposed by the space . . ."

How awful, Grace thinks, that talented designers cannot begin to communicate with words. She compares the original brochure with her final copy and wonders why she finds words for architects easy to craft when she started with little to no knowledge of architecture.

Not the thing, but the perception of thing.

There is that voice again. Perhaps Andy's right, calling her his crazy Hong Kong cousin.

"You were going to be a writer, remember?"

Why is it Juliana remembers, but she doesn't?

*

because she hasn't wanted never wanted to face the fact that yes she is crazy always has been crazy not crazy in the sickopsycho sense but crazy for keeping the lid on. that one day in the manuscript she let loose on the insanity of being chinese and catholic and western and hong kong and american and female and male and virgin and whore. and life and death. that one day in the manuscript she glimpsed if only just for a moment that her perception of thing was never is never would never be the thing as perceived by anyworld she lived in that she

*

Let's go back to reality.

For days, Grace cannot dismiss the image of the butcher block.

Her parents call.

Her father asks. "Are you making enough money?"

Her mother asks. "When are you coming back to see us?"

"I'm sorry I haven't written," Grace says.

Her father declares. "Time magazine claims that there are a growing number of single people households in America."

"When will you marry a rich man?" Her mother repeats the lifelong serious-joke to the girls.

Grace says. "I don't know if I want to stay in America."

"Make sure you get your citizenship first!" Mum insists.

"You don't plan to go back to Paris again, do you?" Dad begins. "Not more of that Bohemian life?"

"Maybe the novel makes her think she should be a writer again," Dad, the thwarted-as-a-violinist-father-breadwinner says to Mum.

"Grace, writing is very difficult. You're better doing your consulting work," Mum, the thwarted-in-her-medical-career-mother-wife says. "Remember, when you first came back from America, I told you you have to get a job first and when you settle down, then you can write?"

"A-Ba, A-Ma, better not spend too much money on this call. I'll say goodbye now."

"Okay, dear. *Kung Hei Fat Choy.*" Her parents wish her together for the new year.

"Yeah," she replies.

After she hangs up, she wonders what her parents would say if they knew the legal, semi-legal, and almost illegal means she used to live and work in Paris, and now in America.

Just before she immigrated to New York, Grace screamed for many days.

No one heard her screams.

The silent screams of the normal neurotic. One interracial marriage. One divorce. One attempted rape by a colleague. One abortion. One suicide attempt.

Just the typical adventures of the average self-proclaimed feminist of the latter part of the twentieth century from a part of the world where feminism isn't "necessary." Everywoman wants "a relationship." Nowoman wants a "bad" relationship. In fact, "no relationship is better than a bad relationship."

As far as Grace is concerned, so much for relationships.

*

she is nowoman not everywoman but still woman. that she is experiencing not jet lag but race lag woman lag culture lag that is catching up. that she wrote "sun days" and then attempted to live "sun days" between eighteen and thirty to find not Anny's nausée but a dance with a skeleton the only ecstasy left.

the fourth copy returns not as gwai gu *not to haunt but to remind of possibilties of options even though this is yet another option in a series of options must she really explore all try all is this what a romantic disposition is all about*

*

Grace Hsu dances in the privacy of her Manhattan home with an invisible partner. "He" died many years ago in the middle of a manuscript.

Andy calls her all the time these days, wondering what has happened to his Hong Kong cousin. Grace has been difficult to reach, recalcitrant. She isn't the laughing, crazy, adaptable cousin anymore of whom he is so proud. Perhaps New York has gotten the better of her. The last time they spoke, she snapped his head off, saying he was an egocentric, sexist, American male who should know better since he's *Chinese* American. None of which makes much sense to him. At least, he doesn't think it should make much sense to him.

Andy consults his friend Jim the psychiatrist and describes these symptoms of irrational behavior, all of which stem from, he is sure, the appearance of that manuscript.

Does she have a boyfriend? Jim asks.

Andy isn't sure. Grace doesn't tell anyone much about her love life, although he's sure she has one. She does occasionally mention dating.

Does she have friends?

Oh yes, Andy says, she has lots of friends and always has. She's the outgoing, friendly type.

Does she write poetry or paint or something? Is she the temperamental artistic type?

Andy doesn't think she's temperamental at all, but thinks she does write a little on the side, but only a little.

Is there a history of mental instability, of imbalance? His friend inquires politely. Andy doesn't know. Chinese people don't talk about these things, he says.

But, says Jim, this is America. Here we talk about these things.

Yes, says Andy, he knows.

*

In her Manhattan apartment, Grace dances with invisible partners. The book lies open at the Munch drypoint.

In America, her professor had said, we talk about these things.

Yes, said Grace, she knew.

Yes, says Grace, she knows. That's why she returned.

Let's end with And She Lived Happily Ever After In The Castle.
At least for now.

RAGE

Five years later (you had to be sure, didn't you besides warmth and tenderness deserve to be rekindled don't they, besides time heals and changes everything in the meandering river of life doesn't it etc.?) you called him from New York to let him know you'd left Hong Kong and that his advice about joining the professional women's group had been good and that now your career as an Asian marketing specialist was taking off to new and unbelievable heights. Oh his voice, his voice was as rapturous as it had been in Hong Kong as he tells you how wonderful it is to hear from you and did you know his company had recently entered into a joint venture with a Hong Kong company whose offices were based in New York and you exclaimed but we must get together let me know when you're next in town and he calls a week later (you wonder at this coincidence but are delighted anyway) to get on your calendar.

The white tablecloths at One Hudson Cafe on West

Broadway in Lower Manhattan are cleaner and crisper than those at Au Trou Normand on Hanoi Street in Kowloon and now the Francophile in you has waned and you are less charmed much less charmed when he remembers the wine and orders the exact same vintage and steers all the conversation away from his wife and over to you. Yet your mind is racing, not listening not wanting to listen to him and you're thinking since he listened before surely now he will listen again and treat you with the same seriousness as he did then when he listened to you talk about your work, your career, your aspirations, your desires.

But the conversation is hesitant and staccato as he replays the incident of the bomb warning in Manila which you had forgotten about since there were always bomb warnings in Manila so why should that one have been special . . . he recalls the white suit you wore the persistence with which he courted you the game, playing the game how important and necessary it was and how he's thought about you again and again and again over the years, you veer off track slightly and ask if he ever received your card congratulating him on his wedding he says yes thanks and returns to that day five years ago in Manila.

Five years ago, he thanked you for the meal the last supper you had prepared (nothing fancy you were always a basic cook) and made pointed but sentimental references to house and hearth and out of the blue he looked at you with his youngest son brown eyes that smiled-cried so beautifully and said some day you'll make someone a good wife and you almost cried but didn't because the one thing that didn't happen during this great romance, this luscious, overblown, sensual, adventurous, four day romance, was that you never cried, at least, not with him.

Now the conversation starts and stops and you wish he weren't in New York especially when he says he has to go check into his hotel because he hasn't done so and he looks at you with an endearing and meaningful smile and you know he expects an invitation to your apartment so you make the excuse that you've had some work done today and the place is a mess and he says of course, I'm sorry, I'm rushing you it isn't fair it has been five years as if as if . . . and he takes your hand and the power repulses you because because . . . but you put that aside because although you now understand a great deal more about what kind of woman you are you still do not understand the advent of rage as it augments inside. So by the second day of his stay in New York, of what must be his purposely concocted business trip the hotel room expense for which he must be paying for out of his own pocket . . . .

So perhaps it was fate after your first night together that your trip to Singapore was cancelled because of a screw up in the new ad campaign launch that insisted, no demanded, that you remain at headquarters in Hong Kong. And he was still there when you called at nine thirty, the minute you knew you would be in town that night, there in his hotel room at the Hilton, because he had forgotten his briefcase (how often in his thirty two years had he ever forgotten his briefcase?) so he had to return to his room and the phone rang and he picked it up because he thought it might be his supplier although as a rule he did not answer ringing telephones when he was in a hurry or so he said. And he was delighted, genuinely pleased to hear from you — you could hear the rapture in his voice when he said all right, tonight at seven, I'll tell them I won't need the car (you still quiver at the long a in car, that funny Bostonian a) — and you thought seven would give you enough time to rush home, shower and change into something scrumptiously sexy because he was that kind of man and you were that kind of woman of almost but not quite thirty or at least you were then five years ago.

And then a week has passed and you're off the cloud and finally returning calls from poor Alistair who wants to know where the hell were you didn't you remember the party and you feel terrible for the poor dear because he can't help being a prig. But you flit right past Alistair and the day until evening when a postcard is in your mailbox from Tokyo which was his next stop and it's short and concise but replete with deeper meanings. You read it, the card, again and again and again, despising all the time the Harlequin romantic feelings bulging up inside, god knows you've cried over his departure even though when you met him he was just another . . . .

In the meantime Alistair, who deserves better treatment than this, but who is (isn't he?) such the perfect escort all the time anytime being so very British (albeit Cambridge not Oxford) which is perfect for the Brits you work with who tolerate your Americanized Chinese state bred of an American university education which they accept but do not respect so long as you date a Chinese or a Brit, in the meantime Alistair is actually exhibiting signs of jealous suspicions since your secretary did mention that no, he's wrong, Miss Lo was in Hong Kong on Thursday and Alistair ever certain that schedules are made to be kept said no, no, she must be mistaken because Miss Lo was supposed to be in Singapore and surely that's where she was but Nancy was adamant and said no Miss Lo was in Hong Kong but she was in meetings all day. Now Alistair is all in a state, inquiring insistently (it would be out of character for him to demand) just what may he ask might be happening surely as important as her job was this intelligence operation style secrecy was well, just a bit too much, wasn't it? And you say oh Alistair don't be tiresome, tiresome being one of those excellent British words you've learnt to use when you simply can't be bothered to answer.

But it doesn't matter what Alistair thinks because time flies etc. until his letter arrives from Africa where he, profligate youngest son of a long established New England family concern (new English is so much nicer than old English you think) waxes lyrical about his travels in the East and you realize his words are surprisingly not corny and yes, quite lyrical, and best of all, his observations about doing business in Asia are filled with insight, bypassing all stereotypes, and probably completely ignored by any American head office concern to which he must report, he being profligate but moderately useful and otherwise ignobly ignorable . . .

Afterwards, the first time afterwards, when he has been more than just another in a long list of others who traipse in and out of your life when you let them this independent high handedness seeming just the right attitude for you, the only Chinese woman to have made manger at the *hong* the

Chinese-British multinational company where your having an MBA is still a strange, untouchable and difficult-to-understand thing . . . afterwards you fall back contented, sated and thoroughly surprised because, well, he just didn't look like someone who could meet your profligate demands despite his abundant nature. He doesn't say much he's just content to be in your bedroom rather than in some hotel room or stuck in the first class lounge at Manila International where you met while security men searched for the non-existent bomb which perpetrated the warning that held up the flight for some six hours.

But the problem is (oh there must be a problem — because romance is not romance whether Harlequin or a more exalted plane version — without a problem) was that his pickup line was so straightforward it wasn't even a pickup line, he made no, absolutely no attempt to get to know you, smooth talk his way through, pretend he was interested in Asia, compliment you on how beautiful you were and what lovely black hair you had . . . no he just ignored his traveling companion (some man whom you can barely picture) and looked at you as if he were a little boy and you some great magical toy in a window he had just fallen in love with and had to have. While you flinched, just a little, under his scrutiny, you sized him up as relatively uninteresting and not worth pursuing though you had pursued (confess, pursuit is half the fun) far less interesting looking men before simply because they were there or you happened to be bored or in the course of stemming the flow of lava. While you flinched he said something you don't even remember what he said and now that you try to remember you don't recall a thing because frankly, you weren't paying attention for once to a possible pick up because you were just about fed up of playing your stupid little games of bed and breakfast in foreign cities at least not since Bahrain when some Romeo had to leap out your hotel room window (how fortunate you were only on the second floor) to ward off his client standing outside your hotel door knocking and begging to be let in to satisfy some Lebanese, macho whim since you know, as he knows, the only attraction you aroused was because you said no.

He said and will you have dinner with me in Hong Kong but you can't remember what preceded the "and" and you replied why should I because for once you really had stopped to question why indeed you should have dinner with this perfect stranger where previously having dinners with perfect strangers filled the diary of your nights, yes just this once you were stopping five minutes longer than usual to think about this life you had acquired for yourself, not too critically but perhaps a trifle regretfully because the likes of an Alistair in between what other lovers you could bump into just didn't do anymore, yes you were telling yourself you are not as completely amoral as you pretend to be or as dreadfully hardened as you like to think you are because your actions, if conventional wisdom is at all wise, are frightening when exposed but meaningless in eternity . . . Alistair being almost as immoral as you as he escorts half naked English models to British parties in Hong Kong to which you have not and will never be invited except as the date of an Englishman, Alistair who dates you when it is convenient to him just as you date him when it is convenient to you to have a foreign devil escort, not mind you, that Larry, the American equivalent of Alistair, is any better although he is taller, more handsome and less tedious than Alistair and in between all this your parents wonder why you never have a Chinese boyfriend (even though they told you go West young woman they expected you would stay West where your forays among Western men can been heard of but not seen and where, especially in America, it is quite fashionable and acceptable to engage in cross cultural sex).

Afterwards you do not light a cigarette or sip more wine since that's only in books or the movies you just lie there because it is comfortable to be horizontal and for a minute for a second the great romance is love even if only for a minute.

Six months later you get a postcard in which he says he's getting married and you don't know what to do about your feelings or even whether or not to believe any feelings of sadness or wistfulness because now that time has passed you have merrily fallen back into your old, unquestioning ways because the impetus to question was out of sight out of mind or at least in Boston which is about as faraway as you can get and you and he never wrote after the first fortnight because really was there anything to say?

The postcard sits around for a day or so as you try to recall the romance the feeling and the white tablecloths at Au Trou Normand which is the only French country cuisine restaurant you know of in Kowloon (even though he was staying on the island you wanted to be closer to home so that the taxi ride would be cheaper for you in case dinner was a disaster). But dinner wasn't a disaster at all because he was a youngest son and youngest sons have a tendency to worship women and treat them like queens which he did you which you ate up because you did you do you always wanted worshippers not lovers the former being far easier on your heart than the latter . . . but worship aside he was a stranger which meant he had no notions no prejudices and took everything you said at face value which is hard to get from friends and other non-strangers.

You talked, don't you always want to do most of the talking which is why you're always at the brink of many a romantic catastrophe because you go out with these men and pretend to listen when in fact you want to talk and they wind up doing all the talking but letting you listen because it does them good and how many (oh don't count the numbers will stagger you) men have told you that you have a man's mind as if that were a compliment and you, oh yes it was your own fault, you lapped it up because that way you never were at a loss for dates thus preventing a repeat of lonely Saturday nights. So you talked and talked and he listened and empathized (you would have despised sympathy) and gazed at you with worshipful eyes until you knew, despite yourself, that you were about to fall in love for a short time in your life.

And afterwards, the second time, he held you and said you are the warmest dearest woman in the world and you heard in that "woman" the meaning of your existence as if he were coaching you for a rebirth, sometime in the future, when being a woman would have much less to do with sex and a lot more to do with love and every trite folly attendant to love.

When he left you by the subway the morning after the second time you floated into work and for once were not preoccupied by your job except to do your job the way a job should be done without the agony. You showed him to nobody you told him to nobody you kept him your secret even afterwards when it was over, gone, utterly finished forever (or so you believed) you didn't even tell your closest girlfriend who had always been a willing listener to all the stories of your escapades.

And he asked, what will you say when one day we meet on a street in Boston and you are with your husband and I am with my wife you said I don't know and he said I'd introduce you and you'd introduce me and we'd tell our spouses we knew each other through work in Hong Kong many moons ago and then we'd walk away after our polite encounter and that would be that. And you said that's right that's the way it would be because that was the way it had to be.

In the end you pen a note at first with tongue-in-cheek intent which says if his marriage doesn't work out to give you a call but you tear this up and pen the conventional politesse offering congratulations and all that and best wishes and whatnot because by now you are smiling and savoring tender memories since tenderness is in high demand but low supply these days and eminently eminently more bankable, storable and memorable than . . . .

You spill wine and excuse your clumsiness and signal time out for a run to the bathroom the time out being in context since you are now anchored in the West where your parents can hear of but not see the Chinese American men you date who all love football and baseball and that other kind of ball out of which time tends to find its way. If only if only you think the conversation could course and surge and be just right even though the sneaking premonition is that it can't possibly be just right and after all you had told yourself in no uncertain terms that you had no designs on him when you called and you did wait, didn't you, till a whole year had passed here in New York before you called?

Even as you doubt you wonder if that maybe he was IT all the time since this was the one love the one secret that you bore for years without revelation and after all it was you, wasn't it, who came to the States and looked him up although you told yourself this was just friendship one of those things etc.?

You suddenly think you don't want to be worshipped by anyone anymore but the damndest thing is that you didn't do a thing about eradicating worship during the intervening five years because, well because there never was time there was always so much travel and in the end there were always so many others who willingly traipsed in and out of your life with no pain no gain no intimacy wrenching horrors of relationships, and the tenderness was soothing was comforting and easily mistakable for love, especially with perfect strangers. On top of all this, the Alistairs and Larrys were replaceable and yes in their own way tender even if these days they arrived in the form of Wall Street investment bankers with names like Hank Ho and were a little less tender but equally as perfect escorts as Alistair and Larry but all the time you never reckoned with the catch up of frenzy, fury, ire, outrage, the catch up of metamorphoses, of rupture, of change.

But Harlequin not a higher plane dictates in moments of luscious surrender and so you say all right and he visits and afterwards you know it was all wrong and he knows too and this has nothing to do with anything because of course two civilized people know when they've made a mistake and are big enough to acknowledge the error put it behind and move on etc. and you're only on the verge but not yet completely unreasonable and youngest sons are not only profligate but prodigal and perpetually apologetic thanks to their warm brown eyes . . .

Afterwards, after the last time, after he's gone, this time for good, the rage erupts.

ALLEGRO QUASI UNA FANTASIA
from: *Concerto in a Major Key*

Yvette Chan awoke, and remembered the bandage on her right hand. She looked around the London hotel room. A distressing beginning, she thought, as she crept quietly out of bed in order not to awaken Mother. Father in the adjoining room was still asleep. Despite the problem her hand presented to piano practice, Yvette was grateful to be in London, away from Ah Yee back in Hong Kong. Finally, she was rid of her *amah*, her nursemaid-woman-in-waiting. At nineteen, she was too old for that outdated Chinese custom, fashionable though it was in Mother's view, for girls from better homes to have *amahs*.

In the bathroom, she undid the bandage. A mere bruise! Yet Mother had insisted — Mother always insisted on impeding piano practice — that she wrap it up. Yvette remembered Father's expression on board the plane when she bumped her hand. Humor your mother, it said. And she had, silencing Mother, upsetting no one.

No jet lag. She had expected the eleven hour flight through the Middle East to tire her. From the bathroom window, she could just see the park. Was she really in Europe? In less than a week, would she really be a pupil at the Academy, alone, without her parents, or Madeline, her teacher? Once Father and Mother had finally agreed, everything had happened so quickly. And no question of Ah Yee hovering around, chaperoning, getting in the way. This was what she wanted, wasn't it?

Mother called. "Ai Lin?"

"In the bathroom."

"Ai Lin, you're not taking off the bandage, are you?"

Mother's nagging, gently domineering, was even more tyrannical than Ah Yee's. Mother wielded real power, Ah Yee did not.

"No, I'm not," Yvette replied.

"Just one more day, and after that you can play again. You don't want to play today, do you?"

No, she would not want to play today or any day if Mother had her way. That was over now, she reminded herself. She was in Europe.

Later, at breakfast, Father said, "We'll go over to the Academy today, Yvette."

"All right."

Mother said, "Don't you think Ai Lin should have some time to do a little sightseeing? After all, she won't be playing anything for a few days."

"But she must. I didn't send her all the way here to see the sights. She'll have plenty of time for that later."

"Oh but her hand . . ."

"Rubbish. There's nothing wrong with her hand. It's just a small bruise."

"Just because you don't believe in Western medicine, there's no need to inflict your outmoded attitudes on our daughter."

"The Western doctor speaks! My dear, need I remind you you haven't practised in fourteen years?"

"There's no need to . . . "

"Yvette, your darling Ai Lin is going to play . . . "

Yes she is, no she's not. Yvette bent her head over the buttered toast. Didn't her parents realize they were in the Hilton? Here they were, arguing like two street hawkers, except that they kept their voices low. Even after the argument subsided, she heard the echo of their *yes-no-yes-no* from years back, first overheard, later as witness, as if she could take sides.

*

Sometime ago — it seemed only yesterday — Miss Madeline Kwong had said. "Yvette, you must go to Europe."

"But I've been to Europe, and I don't like it."

"That's because you've only gone on one short trip with a touring schedule. What do you really know of London, or Paris? All you know is the hotel room and the recital hall. And you always have your father and that baby *amah* fussing around you."

"She's *not* my 'baby *amah*'!"

How could she play European classical music, Miss Kwong wanted to know, only in Hong Kong? Miss Kwong had been wanting to know that for some years.

"But you do," Yvette objected.

"But I run a school and write the local music column. Besides, I've had my apprenticeship abroad. I still keep an apartment in Paris, you know."

Miss Kwong was single, energetic, in her mid-fifties, and highly independent. Mother said she was too ugly to get married. Yvette only knew that no one in Hong Kong taught music quite the way she did.

Last summer, for the first time, Yvette had toured Europe giving recitals. All arranged by Madeline, with her father's approval, and her mother's disapproval. Mother always had had other plans for her — college in America, for example, in engineering or medicine — despite the piano that loomed so large in all her life. The piano that Mother herself started her on, it being fashionable for girls from better families, etc. Of course, Mother never expected her to be talented, just good.

Her father, on the other hand, knew she was talented. He simply never expected her to be good. It was not until she arrived at Miss Madeline Kwong's music school (after five previous years of lessons), that anyone expected her to be both talented and good.

So now, on her walk through a park she told her parents she must take after breakfast, her hand began to ache. Her hands had always had a life of their own. They played when they wanted to. In the last five years, Madeline ensured they would play on command. As if the music were hers to command!

The trouble was, Madeline wanted her to lose herself in music. "Get rid of the mundane in life," Madeline always said, "and the music will take over." But how, wondered Yvette, could she rid herself of her parents' petty arguments, mundane as they were? She could not say, "Excuse me, Mother and Father, you fight, I'll lose myself in music." Even supposing that did work, what of the demon within that whispered about all those men, Madeline's men?

Forget. The way Madeline chose to live her life need not serve as a model for hers. Madeline could, at fifty something, afford to lose herself in music. She remembered what her friend Eric Wylie used to say: *Madeline doesn't want to be trapped into being a Hong Kong Chinese woman.* Which was why she never married, and indulged in Western music and foreign lovers. But it was easy for Eric to laugh: his Chinese mother was a painter, married to an Englishman, and even more flamboyant than Madeline.

Madeline and Mrs. Wylie. Women unlike Mother. Women who repeated, as often as they could, *the music is your life, Yvette.* They sounded almost like Father, and were women of whom Mother strongly disapproved.

Yvette arrived at the exposed section of the park. Chilly. She clutched her jacket tightly, wondering if she had wandered around long. February here was much colder than at home, and damper. Unfamiliar city. Its curious greyness fostered a vague sense of *déja vu*; the sparse winter greenery made Hong Kong's winters seem lush by comparison. She became gradually aware of a foreign-ness — it wasn't English — that made her more fully cognizant of actually being in London. Perhaps it was the Indian litter picker, or the English "bobby." She wasn't sure. But she knew, she was certain, that this was *not* Hong Kong, that *this* was the beginning of something new.

She let out a sudden exclamation. It seemed as if a pain shot through her hand.

What rubbish. She must be imagining the pain. She slipped her hand into her pocket and encoutered the Key to Miss Madeline Kwong's Paris apparttement, a forgotten last minute present urged on her in case she got "sick of London." Mother had objected strenuously to Yvette going alone to Madeline's place where "god knows *what* sort of people might drop by!" Madeline, when Yvette conveyed Mother's sentiment, laughed and said Hong Kong people had "too much money to waste if they didn't appreciate a free room in Paris which even had a piano." So Madeline, in the midst of airport farewells, had slipped the Key quietly into Yvette's hand and whispered, "You're an adult now."

Since she had begun her walk, Yvette had put her parents right out of her mind. Her never-in-agreement parents, especially where her welfare was concerned. Even now, when everything was supposed to be settled about her staying in London and the Academy, and Madeline's contacts in Paris, even now, they still could not agree. She had a sudden vision of herself at forty, a full fledged concert pianist performing Rachmaninoff on stage, breaking down, while in the background, her parents *yes-no-yes-no* arguments sounded loud and long after their deaths.

Rebellion stirred. Would she forever be Father's performing doll and Mother's adversary? Had she come to Europe simply to buckle down to the rigid schedule Father already had in mind for her? And to listen to Mother's whining, ever present;

even after Mother went home long distance calls would persist. And Madeline! Madeline who wanted her to be an artist, to be bohemian and wild. Who would she be now that she was finally in Europe?

The idea came to her in an instant. She would go to Paris, and disappear. To hell with her parents and Madeline and the piano and Madeline's caustic attitude towards people and life. She would go first thing tomorrow. On that early bird service Madeline had mentioned. What had she called it? The . . . *aeroglisseur*. A marvellous name. It floated right off the tongue, especially the way Madeline said it, in her impeccable French. It was easy to go to Paris from London, Madeline said. Very easy.

She would not think about it anymore, otherwise she would get nervous. Just as she would before a recital, when she thought she would forget all the notes for sure. But she never did. Never. Music was easy. Very easy.

She awoke at four. It would be bleak and chilly outside, she thought, as she dressed quietly. No time though to consider such details. Quickly, she had to go quickly, but without rushing, to Victoria Station.

The hotel receptionist barely glanced at her. Once out on the streets, she found a taxi easily enough. People hampered movement, people like Ah Yee, or her parents. Even Miss Kwong sometimes did, when she interrupted her playing. As the taxi rolled towards her destination, she told herself: Movement is everything.

At the station, Yvette had about forty minutes to spare

before boarding the train to Dover. She bought a newspaper and sat down on a bench. Any newspaper, any bench. No Father, buying the *Times*. No Mother, pointing out, discreetly, that this bench was occupied by an undesirable person, and wouldn't it better to sit on that bench? No Ah Yee, muttering that newspapers were dirty. Yvette bought the first newspaper she saw and sat on a bench. Only after she sat down did she notice that her paper was a two day old *Tribune*.

She read, absorbed in a story about some celebrity sex scandal that resulted in a lawsuit, for a good ten minutes, before she became aware of an uncomfortable sensation against her thigh. It was a foot. The sleeping vagrant who occupied the remainder of the bench had shifted in his sleep. His big toe, sticking out of a hole in his canvas sneaker, jabbed into the folds of her skirt. She got up and moved to another bench, annoyed to find a streak of grime on her light grey skirt.

The wait was already making her impatient. She was still on Ah Yee time — *poco a poco smorzando* was the way she thought of it — which allowed too much time for everything. Too much time for the picayune details of life. And now she had to wait, with nothing better to do except read a two day old newspaper and avoid a vagrant's big toes. The only thing left to do was think.

Which made her think about that dream again, her recurrent dream she did not understand. Last night, she ran along that giant keyboard, chromatically, beginning, as always, from the upper register. White, black, white, black, white, black, white, white. Slowly at first, as she became accustomed to reaching each key, black, then white, then black, until eventually she built up speed, and the run was automatic. All the time, a metronome ticked in the background.

Something about the ticking disturbed her now, as she tried to pull together the pieces of her dream. Strange, but she saw everything for the first time with remarkable clarity. When had the dream begun? She couldn't recall; it seemed to have always been there. But this morning, perhaps due to the strangeness of the day, she heard the chromatic scale, felt the gust of wind past her as she ran, and sensed, with a growing excitement, why the metronome's ticking always, invariably disturbed her.

The dream metronome was much too slow! It ticked away, setting its own tempo and rhythm, at about sixty. But what puzzled her was that she had not known, all this time, how slow it was.

Why?

" . . . Dover!"

Yvette looked at the gate. Her train was preparing to leave. She grabbed her suitcase and ran, barely making it through the gate in time.

"Easy, Miss."

The ticket collector smiled. Yvette felt incredibly foolish, sitting in the station all that time, yet almost missing her train. It would not have happened if she had been with Ah Yee who would have hovered around the gate. Of course, she thought, as she boarded the train, she would hardly be travelling at this hour with Ah Yee. Far away, or so it sounded, a whistle blew.

*

She slept all the way to Dover. No real movement on board the train: just a long rest, until it was time to think again. A surge of people now, towards the *aeroglisseur*. Like boarding a plane, or preparing to play. It was easy. Why did everyone pretend it was so hard?

She chose a window seat and fastened her seat belt. A man sat down beside her. The voice inside her said: Yvette Chan, this is music, nothing else. She shuddered suddenly, and grasped her bandaged hand close to herself.

They took off.

The man said, "What happened to your hand?"

Yvette stared out the window, and did not reply, unaware she had been addressed. She felt a tap on her shoulder.

"Parlez Anglais, Mademoiselle?"

"What?"

How rude of her, she thought, as soon as she'd said it. But he had startled her.

"Oh, you do speak English. I wasn't sure."

She looked at the stranger: a funny looking man. Caucasian, but with Oriental eyes. Intriguing.

He continued, "May I speak to you?"

She saw him look at the hand, still clutched near her breast. Conscious of the slight absurdity of her pose, she dropped her hands to her lap.

"Yes, of course." Unsure of what to say next, she added, "Good morning."

The man smiled. Little wrinkles appeared around his eyes, which, Yvette noticed, were a greyish green. He rubbed his brown-grey beard lightly.

"Good morning. Is your hand hurting you?"

"Oh no, not really."

She waited, wondering: is he just making conversation? And then, the thought: he looks at me as if he sees through my bandage, my glasses, my polite smile.

"I take it you're not from Vietnam."

Before she could stop herself, she said, "What an odd thing to say," and then, "oh no!"

"Oh, that's all right. I'm afraid it is rather an odd thing to say. I confess, I saw you sleeping on the train and you reminded me then of the many Vietnamese I've seen in Paris."

"I'm from Hong Kong."

There was something about this man that puzzled her. Of course, the accent. It sounded so gentle. Not clipped, like the English, or lazy, like the Americans. Perhaps he was French. His voice recalled Marc, the French violinist she had had that very brief affair with a year ago, the one Mother almost caught her with, the one . . .

"What do you do?" he asked.

No, not French. He was much too "fast," as her friend Eric would say. Perhaps American.

"Nothing."

"You have to do something."

"Why? I might just be a schoolgirl for all you know."

"Nope."

"Why not?"

"Too old."

She wanted to laugh out loud, but restrained herself. For once, she wasn't being told how young she looked. Mother, of course, attributed her youthful appearance to the lack of make up and straight hair. And the glasses. But Mother — fashionably coiffured at the hairdresser's each week, perfectly made up each morning, dictated by vanity into those awful contacts — Mother would think that.

"My mother wouldn't agree."

"What does your mother do?

"She's a former doctor and a full time socialite."

This time, he laughed, quited unrestrainedly.

"Is there such a thing?"

"In Hong Kong there is."

"So are you a full time or former?"

"Full time or former what?"

"Schoolgirl."

He said it with such seriousness that she had to smile. He made her feel good, not rushed. This struck her as interesting: men made her feel rushed. Of course, the circumstances in which she always met men were usually highly restrictive, what with . . .

"Well?"

He was waiting for an answer.

"Do you live in Paris?"

"You didn't answer my question."

Well, she wouldn't answer, she decided, not yet. It occured to her that time could go on forever if she wanted it to.

She asked. "Do you know Paris well?"

"Yes."

"Well, here's a bargain. You tell me about Paris, and I'll answer your question." Seeing his puzzled look, she added.

"Promise. You see, I've only been in Paris once before."

He did not speak at once. Yvette wondered if he thought her silly, or too forward. Not that she minded — she felt incredibly unrestrained — but she would rather like to talk about Paris. She hoped she hadn't put him off completely.

And then, he began to hum. She listened to the strange melody. Nothing recognizable. Just the air of something half remembered way in the back of her memory. Phrases, not a whole. But what surprised her most was the feeling of space he conveyed. A big empty space like a hole which, if you tried to look into it, revealed no bottom, no light.

She listened then, as he continued to hum. Paris did not matter, nor their earlier conversation. Even the bandage did not matter. If her hand did ache, she was certain it was an imaginary pain. The *aeroglisseur* could fall into the sea. The world around her might disappear as long as the melody remained.

She closed her eyes and sank into her seat. Yesterday's realities drifted far away. *No-yes-no-yes-no-yes.* Ah Yee cajoling, Ah Yee cackling. And finally Miss Kwong saying, over and over again, *Yvette you are an artist you must, Yvette you are an artist you must, Yvette.*

*

He woke her on board the train to Paris

"Practising hibernation?" He was smiling.

Yvette rubbed her eyes. "How did I get on the train?"

"You walked off the boat and boarded it."

"I did?"

It wasn't possible she couldn't remember. For an instant, she panicked, and pulled out her passport from her purse. The French visa stared back at her, stamped with an entry.

"Was I sleepwalking?"

"I don't think so. We talked about Paris, remember?"

"Yes," she paused, remembering, " and you were humming something."

"Was I? I'm told I do that sometimes."

He frowned, and a note of concern came into his voice. "Are you all right? You look a little pale."

She did not want to say she couldn't remember. Her bandaged hand began to throb, almost imperceptibly. Perhaps it was just fatigue. Perhaps it was like that point in a performance where the soloist paused, and the orchestra took over. Where all she could do was to sit still and let the music take her along until the moment she heard her cue and then.

Now, she turned to him. "I'm okay, just tired. What were we saying about Paris?"

He spent the rest of the journey telling her about a friend of his who lived on a houseboat *sous* le Pont des Arts. Yvette only half listened. She was too preoccupied with trying to remember what had in fact happened since the *aeroglisseur*. At some point in the conversation, he mentioned seeing her in Paris, to which she replied, perhaps.

The train ride seemed extremely short. On arrival at the Gare du Nord, Yvette pulled out the address: 11 Rue Amrobise Paré. Just around the corner from the *gare*, Yvette, Miss Kwong had said. Walking distance.

"I must apologize for not being able to see you to your place. I have a previous appointment."

His apology surprised her. "Oh, that's quite all right. I wouldn't expect you to."

They walked out of the *gare* together.

"I'm going left," he said, adding, "*à gauche*. You must practise your French now."

"And I'm going right."

"So, it's *au revoir*?"

She smiled. "Yes, I have enjoyed our conversation, by the way."

"Good. *Bon*."

He shook her hand, and began to walk away.

She called after him. "Oh say, what's your name?"

"Fava. Leon Fava."

And then she, after turning *à droit*, walked off in search of her new home.

THE SEVENTIES

THE TRYST

1981, January. Sometimes, I dream of Monique. Her voice is very soft as she bites my ear. She has tiny breasts, tinier than mine. The hairs on her legs are smooth, unspoilt by a razor. I start to resist, but she kisses me, whispers, "We are here to serve each other." I submit. My passivity troubles me.

*

I met Monique in 1980 in Taipei, Taiwan. The August morning we met, I arrived at Andre's house, which was in the middle of that city. He was wearing a kimono when he greeted me.

"Come in, come in." He embraced me, kissing both my cheeks. He stepped back to look me over. "I can see why David Markowitz sent you," he said, smiling.

I'm David Markowitz's main woman, in between his typewriter and China. David's an American foreign correspondent, a China-watcher who scurries back and forth between Peking and Hong Kong, where I live. Andre's an

Oriental Art historian from Paris, and David's best friend in Taipei. David has a habit of "sending" me to look up his global friends, which complements my globe scouring life as an English language travel writer. Sort of.

The house was floored by bamboo tatami mats. There were no doors between the rooms. I saw a tiny figure, perhaps a young boy, in the bedroom folding up the covers. Andre was wearing indoor slippers. I removed my shoes.

"Let me make you some tea," he offered. Despite his bulk, Andre moved gracefully. I sat down, cross legged, on the nearest cushion.

"That Da-vid!" Andre pronounced the name, heavily accenting the second syllable. "He has the eye for *la petite femme Chinoise!*"

I smiled, sort of. It was not the first time David's dubious compliments had come back to me via a third party. Little Chinese woman indeed. How much longer, I wondered, would I want David as my main man?

The young boy entered the living room as Andre brought the tea. "He" turned out to be a young woman. Her short cropped dark hair, and loose fitting shirt and pants, had deceived me. But there was little masculinity in her face, except for a very slight boyishness. She had large, extremely round and beautiful eyes.

"*Bonjour.*" She smiled at me. Her tiny mouth pursed slightly, almost imperceptibly.

I smiled back. In contrast to my tan, her skin was pale.

Andre glanced at me. "*Elle ne parle pas francais,* do you?"

I shook my head. "Not enough." I accepted my cup of tea

from Andre with both hands. It was hot. The woman seated herself on the cushion opposite me. "Do you speak English?" I asked.

She replied, "A little."

"She is shy," Andre said, placing his arm around her shoulders. "You must talk to her. I think she would like to practise English with you."

I nodded. I wondered if this were Andre's girlfriend, "the incredibly beautifully Giselle" over whom David often raved.

She extended her hand. "I am Monique."

The phone rang. Andre went to his study to answer it. He was on the phone for almost fifteen minutes. Snatches of expressive Mandarin drifted out to us.

Monique and I looked at each other. I felt quite dumb, quite unlike my usual self. I certainly was not the lively, talkative young woman David had probably said I was. Monique's eyes were really quite startling. I caught myself staring at them, and looked away, embarassed. She did not lower her gaze. I felt drawn to her.

Monique broke the silence. "You expected Andre's friend, Giselle?"

I nodded, surprised.

"She is in Paris. She'll be back tomorrow." Then, seeing my puzzled look, she added, "We are friends, Giselle and I. Andre is both our friends."

I caught the pain in her look as she said that. Woman's pain. For a very brief moment, our eyes locked in sympathy. The moment passed.

"We will be in 'ong Kong next week," she said.

"Really? You must come see me."

"Oh?" Her eyes seemed to widen with pleasure. "Andre will be very busy. Can you show me around?"

"Yes." My reply was rapid, without hesitation.

"Then," she smiled, "we must meet in 'ong Kong."

After Andre returned to the living room, I remained for another hour or so. I regretted having to leave, but I had a plane to catch back to Hong Kong that afternoon. Outside the house, I climbed aboard my motorcycle and switched on the ignition.

"See you in 'ong Kong, per'aps," Andre said.

I waved as I drove away. Yes, I thought. And Monique.

Taipei is a sprawling city, much more spread out than Hong Kong. It's modern enough, I suppose. But it's very Chinese — in history, tradition, and nationalistic spirit. Andre said he chose Taipei for a base because it was so Chinese, and the next best thing to being in China itself. David bitches about China a lot: his vices abhor Communism. I don't like Taipei, and I have no desire to visit Peking at the moment (even though David is based there). I'm much happier here in Hong Kong. When it comes to things Chinese, foreigners always want the real thing. Hong Kong's good enough for me: non-Communist, non-Nationalist. *Laissez-faire* Chinese, at least for now while we're still a British colony.

I was glad to get back home. Two weeks was too long to be in Taipei. Monique had been a high point, making *chez* Andre a worthwhile visit. But I really did not expect to see her or Andre again. Just another of my many typical travel encounters who always said, "see you in Hong Kong."

So I was surprised when, a week after my return, Andre called.

After dispensing with pleasantries, I asked. "Do you know where David is? He's supposed to be here in Hong Kong."

Andre said, "He arrives in Taipei today. A sudden assignment. I leave him to look after Giselle. His cable said to take care of you."

Terrific. Why couldn't David tell me these things himself?

Andre continued, "But first, you must do me a favor?"

"What's that?"

"Look after Monique for me."

It was arranged that Monique and I would have a dim sum lunch together, and Andre would meet us that evening at my place. For the rest of the morning, I was in a state of flux. When Alistair (my British lover in David's absence) called to confirm our dinner date three days hence, I said he would not want to see me. I tried to explain the flux but failed. I could picture him shaking his head.

"Whatever you say. I'll ring next week."

I replaced the receiver. Alistair tolerated my shenanigans involving David and his friends, but he did like life ordered. I wondered why he bothered with me.

Monique was waiting alone at the door of the restaurant. We linked arms and walked in. It was an automatic gesture on my part, something I had not done with another girl since school days. On a hunch, I asked Monique if she had attended an all girls' Convent school. She had. I'm a Convent school mistake myself, Sino-American-missionary style.

The *dim sum* lunch fascinated her. Waitresses patrolled the aisles, pushing carts filled with assorted dishes. She ate everything willingly, even the chicken's feet. The toenails did not appear to faze her.

We talked about France. I was planning a trip to Europe in another month or so. Paris was definitely on my itinerary. She said she was a medical student, and lived outside Paris in Tours. This was her first trip to Asia. Her biggest surprise was that Taipei and Hong Kong were so modernized and Western. She amused me by her observation that Chinese people seemed to be very patient. Was I, I wondered.

Her English, though halting, had a certain lilt, a musicality. The conversation was innocent enough. Hence, she caught me quite unawares when she said,

"You are promiscuous? Andre says you are."

"How does he know?" I retorted.

She giggled like a naughty schholgirl. "Because Andre says Da-vid pre-fairs promiscuous girls. So he doesn't 'ave to get too involved."

David thinks Chinese girls are promiscuous, especially around Western men. Real life versions of Suzie Wong, the Hong Kong prostitute whose romantic American (or was it English?) lover sweeps her away in marriage, to live happily (and unpromiscuously) ever after (as long as they remain in Asia, of course, since Suzie's spoken English is pidgin, at best).

I should have been insulted by Monique's cheek. Instead, I found her expression appealing.

"I like Andre," she said, "but I pre-fair girls."

This sudden confidence arrested me. I felt like telling her

about Alistair, saying yes, I could be called promiscuous because I had my one or two part time lovers to supplement David's perpetual absence. I wanted to ask her if "pre-fairing girls" worked any better, since she was herself Andre's part time lover.

"Don't be angry," she continued, in response to my silence.

"I'm not." There was an uncomfortable pause. What the hell. Experience before moral conflict. "Do you prefer Chinese girls?"

She replied eagerly. "I 'ave never known a Chinese girl."

Her eagerness repelled me. Yet her smile was gentle, the invitation in her eyes unthreatening.

I could hear David questioning me, wanting to know details. Inwardly, I cringed. It seemed this meeting between Monique and me had all been arranged by Andre and David. Surely they (in their liberated sexual wisdom) knew about Monique's "preferences"? But then, David knows me, and feeds my appetite for Occidental-style excitement.

"Have you met David?" I asked.

"No. Andre speaks about him, says he is very intelligent, very charming."

"Yes," I acquiesced, "that he is. Too charming."

"Like Andre?"

"Like Andre," I agreed.

We both laughed. The tension dissolved. She squeezed my hand, and excused herself to the bathroom. In her absence, I found myself thinking that I wasn't patient, just passive. Especially with David. He had too much energy, too much presence. His charm exhausted me. I spent enough energy and charm creating a presence for myself at work (I'm the only Chinese, besides the secretary, on an all Caucasian staff), and for my lovers. Leftover energy I spent waiting for David to show up. By the time he did, I was almost happy to let him take over. Of course, I observed ironically, it was very Chinese to be passive.

When she returned, Monique said, "A man directed me to the men's room."

"Oh!" I exclaimed, indignant. "How stupid of him. Anyone can see you're a woman."

She shrugged. "It has happened before."

We ate till we were quite full.

That evening, Andre arrived at my place to reclaim Monique. He did his two cheek greeting kiss; one hand squeezed my waist, the other just brushed my breast. It figured.

"You have exercised your Chinese hospitality today, *cherie.* Not just 'guest air' I hope." He placed an arm around each of us as he spoke.

"Guest air," I said, referring to the Chinese expression for polite social intercourse, "ends when the person is no longer a guest. You and Monique are both still my guests, aren't you?"

"Ah! David describes your patient nature well," he said as he released me. "Also, your people have such a wonderful tradition of hospitality."

Tradition be damned, I thought, dismissing his enthusiasm. Andre, for all his worldliness, knew exactly when to be naive. He played up the role of "Westerner-enchanted-by -the-East" to the hilt. Just like David, when he wanted his way. Perhaps, I wasn't so different: I was enchanted by Western freedom, by a Western way of life, especially since it meant I could abandon Chinese culture and tradition with impunity, when it suited me.

Monique said in French, "We have been all over 'ong Kong today. She is an excellent guide."

Andre nodded and smiled at me.

"Practice," I said. "Let's drink some *sake*."

I served the Japanese wine. Steam rose from the funnel of the tiny, earthenware carafe. We sat on my sheepskin rug. Andre conversed volubly. He was indeed, as Monique and I earlier agreed, charming.

Dinner was rice, Chinese cabbage soup, and squid cooked with black mushrooms. I had enjoyed preparing it for my guests: tradition of hospitality, I guess. We laughed a lot while we ate. After the meal, Andre went to the bathroom. Monique immediately stroked my bare arm. I felt goosebumps rise.

She whispered. "You 'ave not forgotten?"

I felt ridiculously childish, unable to free myself from this social intrigue into which I had been drawn. "No," I replied.

Andre was more than friendly the rest of the evening. He occasionally touched my hair and neck; once he even rubbed my thigh. Why couldn't I simply say *stop, enough of this charade, I've had it with David and his friends?* I owed Andre and Monique nothing. Yet I submitted, helped on by the sake. I was fascinated by the situation, and Monique's large, beautiful eyes. I belonged in this game, in this temporary triangle. As surely as I belonged in the world peopled by

Andres, Moniques, Alistairs. And David.

At one a.m., Andre said, "We must go."

I nodded, wishing it were true.

"Unless, of course, you would like us to stay?"

I shrugged. He looked at Monique, who shrugged also. He stepped back and surveyed the two of us.

"Monique!" He sounded angry, accusatory.

She looked away from him. "*Rien*," she said, indifferently.

A French exchange followed. It was much too rapid for me to understand. Andre towered over her. I understood him to say something like "not again."

The easiest thing to do, I decided, was ignore them. I proceeded to lay out blankets and pillows on the sheepskin rug. Chinese practicality, David would say.

"Goodnight," I said from the doorway of my bedroom. Monique caught my eye briefly before I shut the door. I climbed into bed, emotionally fed up, So much for cross cultural communication. I dozed off while they quarrelled.

It was three a.m. by my bedside clock when she crept into my bed. I got up and locked the bedroom door. As the lock clicked, I heard Andre swear softly.

Andre returned to Taipei, leaving Monique with me. He was very good humoured about it by morning. Sophisticated. Thought it *merveilleux* that Monique and I got it off together. He didn't understand that there was more to it than getting off.

Monique and I spent a week together. Mostly, we talked, although we made love a couple of times. I confessed to my innate heterosexuality. She shrugged.

I talked a little about David and me, about how busy he always was with his work. He was jealous, I said, of Alistair and my other lovers (I suspected he had one or two flings, but no other regular lover). Yet he was never around to spend time with me.

Monique said of me, "You too are a busy girl."

To avoid boring her with all this, I chose to tell her stories about Asia instead. She seemed particularly interested in the story of Suzie Wong, since she had neither seen the movie nor read the novel. I said it was a rather romanticized idea of a Hong Kong prostitute, and that it could give the wrong idea about Hong Kong women. Monique smiled and said prostitutes fell in love too.

By the end of the week, Monique had told me a lot about herself. Her sexual experiences always seemed to revolve around the *menage à trois*. She was afraid of being a complete lesbian, she said. Sometimes, we talked all night long. Often, she laughed. But I know she cried. Quiet, secret tears she thought I couldn't hear. The last morning of her stay, she fell asleep in my arms, after she had finally cried her tears to me.

I did not miss David that week.

*

1982. The dream returns less often now that winter's here.

I never saw Monique again after that week. I did receive one letter, months after her departure. She told me she had become completely lesbian. "Andre always preferred two girls," she wrote, "sometimes more. Giselle was my good friend, and I trusted her. But the friends do not always choose the right way, for themselves, or their friends. Perhaps I must thank you for helping me discover my own way, because you take me honestly as a lesbian and friend.

"You are right to say that I should not give in to Andre's 'triangular' love. The story I like best is the one you tell me about the Chinese tradition of concubines, that Chinese men show their wealth by having one wife and many concubines. Perhaps Andre is too long in a Chinese country? And David too? They worship too much the old Chinese traditions, and forget they belong to the West.

"But you, you are not Suzie Wong or a Chinese man. Why must you act like either? You are too patient with men — they do not love you, only your sex. It is a pity you cannot be lesbian too."

She added an open invitation to visit her in France.

I didn't tell David about Monique and me, since I figured Andre would. For some reason, Andre didn't. Maybe he wasn't so happy about it after all.

I moved to Paris this summer, and put David-as-lover completely behind me. He drops the occasional line, in pursuit of my peregrinations (as he calls them). He is as witty, amusing, and charming on paper as he is in person. Which makes him a troublesome memory, since he is the most romantic American I know.

Last night, I dreamt about Monique again. She begins to make love to me; Andre and David watch, amused. I say "stop," but my voice dies away. All three surround me: David smiles, Andre smiles, Monique brushes her tiny lips across my cheek. I look up, above their heads towards the empty air. The air is whispering: "you have not forgotten?" in my own voice. Then slowly, slowly, I fade out. Like a specter. My passivity does not trouble me.

DANNEMORA

Mrs. Joyce Camden straightened the painting, returned to the vinyl sofa, and lit a cigarette.

Her husband Edward said, "Why don't you tell Michael and Diana where you got that painting from?"

They were entertaining friends of his from his former RAF days. Her steamed fish dinner had not failed. Edward had made everyone recoil and laugh at the same time by pretending to eat the eye. It was funny about the British: no matter how long they lived in Hong Kong, they never became quite accustomed to seeing such things as the fish served whole.

Joyce sipped her San Miguel. "Do you really think anyone wants to hear about that, Edward?" she asked.

"Of course, love. Come on, it's a good story."

She gazed at the painting. It seemed she hadn't looked at it properly for a long time. A vase of dried flowers against a plate on a stand. An oil, in an olive colored wood frame. Funny, but she'd forgotten how nice it really was.

"I got it in America," she began, "from an inmate at Dannemora named Fred Jefferson."

"An inmate? Not really?" Diana exclaimed.

"Really. I used to visit Dannemora when I was a college student. The foreign student office would send me." Seeing their smirk, she added, "To give talks about Hong Kong, you see. Anyway, Fred was a painter — he made a living from his work while he was in there — and we started writing letters to each other. One day, he said he wanted to give me this painting because he thought it was 'Oriental.'"

Her husband interrupted. "Bollocks. It's not the slightest bit Oriental at all."

"I know, but that's what he said."

"But why would you visit a prisoner, or write him?" Diana asked. "You hadn't known him previously, had you?"

"No, I hadn't. It wasn't like a prison. More of a rehabilitation centre."

"Some rehabilitation," snorted Edward. "The bloke wanted Joyce to take some jewellery out of there. Taking advantage of the acquaintance, he was. Of course, she was only nineteen then."

"And did you do it?" asked Michael.

"No, of course not!" she retorted.

The conversation turned to reminiscences of Air Force days in Bahrain. Joyce remained quiet, feeling somewhat insulted. She knew they thought America strange, although they didn't actually say so. Even Edward thought that. None of them had ever been there, nor had they any desire to go. It seemed too difficult explaining why she, a Hong Kong Chinese, would spend four years on her own at an American university studying English Literature, and visiting a prisoner. Besides, she was tired of explaining herself all the time.

*

"Diana was laughing at me tonight, wasn't she?"

Edward switched off the bedside light, and turned towards her. "Why d'you say that?"

"She's a bitch. I don't think she likes me. She's one of those who doesn't believe in associating with 'the Chinese.' The only reason she does is because of you."

"Oh go to sleep. You're being over sensitive." He kissed her and rolled over.

Joyce lit a cigarette, and lay awake for the next couple of hours. How easy for Edward to sleep! Nothing ever bothered him. During their one year of marriage, they saw his friends, drank at his pubs, and lived his Hong Kong. Oh, she didn't mind; she even preferred it that way. But it was funny not feeling at home in her own city. Two years ago in '74, she'd graduated, come home, found Hong Kong dreadfully confining, and almost gone straight back to graduate school even though that idea revolted her. Anything to get away from living at home, and listening to family and old friends joke about how "Americanized" she'd become as if it were a disease. Then, she'd met Edward. When he proposed, he reminded her: you're not an American, Joyce. She stayed, knowing he was right.

After her third cigarette, she finally began to feel sleepy. Curling up next to her husband, she closed her eyes. This was home, she thought, as she drifted off. This was home now.

*

Her mother called at work the next morning to remind her of her father's birthday the next day.

"I hadn't forgotten," she replied curtly. But right away, she thought of the expense. Why did Dad's birthday have to be at the end of the month? If only she were paid weekly, as she had been in America.

"You're both coming to dinner, aren't you?"

"Yes, yes."

"Really Joyce, no need to be impatient. How's Edward?"

"Fine. Listen Mum, I have to get back to work."

For the rest of the day, she tried to concentrate on her latest assignment: a new sun tan oil commercial to be directed at the "young, modern, westernized locals" who watched the English language channels. In other words, locals like herself. She rubbed a little oil on her arm and smelled it. Uninspiring.

The account executive popped his head in around mid afternoon and said, "Whatever we do, we don't want to use a *gwaipo* model for this commercial."

She winced. Her husband was a *gwailo* after all. A foreign devil man. Sometimes, her Chinese colleagues forgot this when they talked to her about foreigners. Still, whose problem was that? Looking up from her typewriter, she said, "I've decided to look for a Eurasian girl or an indeterminate Asian. How's that?"

He thought a moment. "Might work. Just make sure she doesn't have *gwai* wrinkles like the last girl." With that, he disappeared.

Joyce reached for her telephone index to find the model agency's number. She liked her job in this Chinese run advertising agency, and her colleagues. Honestly, she did. She could go far in a career with this experience. If only . . . She sighed, and dialed. If only Hong Kong weren't Hong Kong, she thought, as she listened to the telephone ring.

*

In the evening, she searched in Daimaru, the Japanese department store near her office, for an inexpensive but presentable gift. Birthdays were a nuisance when money was tight. Not having the patience to fight the crowds, she settled on a bottle of scotch. Her mother wouldn't be pleased, but it was Dad's birthday.

"Hello, Joyce," she heard an English voice say, as she was fumbling with her purse at the cashier. She looked up and saw Nigel, Edward's friend who was a chartered accountant.

"When are you and Edward going to stop by for a drink? You mustn't let those dogs out in the country keep you away from us city people, you know."

She smiled. It still seemed comical to her that Edward trained dogs for a living. Their village house was also a kennel for dogs of mostly expatriate customers who went back to England or elsewhere for their six week home leave.

"We'll be by, Nigel. Doing some shopping, are you?"

"Yes. I need some new shirts. I haven't got a local wife who knows Hong Kong to shop for me like some lucky devils."

It was then she looked at Nigel's clothes. A well tailored, conservative gray suit, matched by an expensive silk tie and fancy shirt. Nigel, like so many expatriates, did rather well in

Hong Kong. She and Edward didn't do badly at all, but compared to someone like Nigel, their unfurnished 600 sq. ft. home with a tile floor and exposed wiring was slumming. But Edward was working class. He didn't have professional qualifications or a university degree. There wasn't a foreign company absorbing an exorbitant rent for a large two bedroom flat in a posh area. But this was Hong Kong, she thought, and dismissed her thoughts about how different it would be if they lived in America.

"Edward's getting to be quite a local," Nigel was saying. "The last time I called, he answered in Cantonese."

Joyce laughed. "He's got to practice, you know. The villagers don't speak any English."

"Well, I'll be seeing you, Joyce. Give Edward my regards." He kissed her and wandered off into the crowds.

Nigel was sincere, she thought, as she paid for the scotch. Despite their class difference, he didn't look down on Edward. There were times she wished she had married an expatriate like Nigel. Of course, she'd never have met him if it weren't for Edward, Hong Kong being what it was . . .

Oh, where could such thoughts possibly lead? For the first time, Joyce realized how tired her days made her feel.

*

Her father's birthday dinner went smoothly enough, and was even quite enjoyable. Edward and Dad always got along fairly well, once Dad had accepted that the marriage would take place whether or not he approved of it. The two of them drank and joked. But, mused Joyce, Dad was a businessman, which meant he got along with everyone.

After dinner, she lit up a cigarette.

Her mother commented. "Smoking a lot, aren't you, dear?"

"Mum, please."

"Bad American habits," Edward interjected.

He was joking, of course, since he himself smoked, but tonight, she resented it. Everyone, it seemed, did something she resented. She pouted in silence.

"How's the dog business, Edward?" asked her father.

"All right, I suppose. It's a living."

Joyce saw her mother frown, and waited in anxious anticipation for the remark that was sure to follow. It did.

"Edward," began her mother, in the tone Joyce thought of as "Mum just saying this for your own good." "Have you thought about taking some business courses, maybe at the Polytechnic?"

"Mum . . . " Joyce's voice held a warning.

"Can't say I have," said Edward. "Never did like school. Besides, I'm not going back to school with a bunch of locals. Wouldn't do for us *gwailos*, would it?"

Joyce saw the laugh in her husband's eyes as he said this.

But Mum continued, undaunted. "Surely you don't want to just train dogs?"

"He does run a kennel, Mum," Joyce said.

"Yes, but he could learn about business management if he'd just take some courses. I'm only suggesting it for both your own good."

Her father cleared his throat. "Anyone want some brandy?"

"Don't mind if I do," Edward responded.

Joyce sighed in exasperation. In a way, her mother was right.

But Edward was Edward, with no pretensions whatsoever. Whom she loved. What difference did it make what he did?

Her mother bustled off after dinner, leaving her alone with Dad and Edward. They were talking about colonialism again. It was amazing, Joyce thought, how alike Edward and her father were. They were both men of leisure, passively acquiescent to life's incongruities. They could talk for hours over brandies and cigars, or just sit in silence. Really, she decided, they were eminently suited to Hong Kong, the last of Britain's colonies, where time seemed borrowed from an earlier, more gracious era of unquestioned racism. That is, as long as you were English, or "educated" in the Occidental mode, as her father was.

"And the sun is setting on the British Empire, though I hope it's after I'm dead," her father was saying.

Edward and Dad, thought Joyce, were thoroughly enjoying themselves.

"Which is why I've got to keep me end up before it does — you know, *mem sahib* and all that — isn't that right, girl?"

"Oh honestly," she said, "you two are the most god awful bores."

"It's all that American university learning, isn't it?" He addressed her father with a wink. "Makes her think she knows more than everyone else."

Any other time, she could have laughed it off. None of it mattered, not really. But tonight . . . she got up and joined her mother in the kitchen. Her father frowned.

*

Later, at home.

"You're tense, girl."

"Oh, leave me alone."

"The job getting to you?"

"You know that's not the case."

She hated it when he brought up her job. Was it her fault she could earn more money than him? Why did he have to be such a pig about it?

"You're doing too much. You can't work all day and run the house as well."

"And your bloody business."

"I said I'd take care of things, didn't I?"

"You talk and talk about expanding. But you don't even put your books in order. Now we've got cases of dog food cluttering up the place, and you haven't even started an inventory. If I didn't take care of all that, who would?"

"You do your job, and I'll do mine."

"Oh really? What about the 'help' you were to give me with the housework?"

"I do dishes."

"Two days later."

She saw his face relax as he shook his head. "Joyce, are we going to argue about all that again? Can't we just watch the telly and not fight?"

"The telly, the telly! All you want to do is drink and watch telly! Can't we ever do anything else?"

"Like what?"

"Oh, go to a play, swimming, something."

She saw his jaw hardening, giving his countenance that rare look of confidence she now recognized.

"You do something. I'm going to more pleasant company."

He grabbed his jacket and left. Joyce heard the motorcycle roar die away down the road. More pleasant company indeed! Getting drunk at his Sai Kung pub. Mouthing off to those washed up expats who couldn't leave Hong Kong, and the comfort of their white superiority. If Edward were in England, he'd be lucky if he could live half as well as he did now. The unfairness of it all! Even his "business" wouldn't have gotten started if she hadn't pitched in her money. In fact, the only reason he'd managed to drift from job to job for seven years after leaving the Air Force was, was . . .

Because he was English!

She began to cry. What did it matter what the world was like? It was awful of her to be racist and unfair. Hadn't she told Edward she loved him no matter what he was or did? Hadn't Edward helped her make some sense of the confusion she felt when she first returned to Hong Kong, and felt hopelessly out of place? Edward was her husband, whom she'd freely chosen, over whom she'd fought fiercely with her parents to marry. These frustrations and angry feelings had nothing to do with race, had they?

Joyce went to the bedroom and began to undress. If only she could take a hot bath! But all they had was a cold shower, these village houses being somewhat ill equipped. Of course, she had wanted to "rough it" over her mother's objections. Well, what else could she and Edward afford? Rents here weren't sensible like in America.

"You're in Hong Kong now, girl!" she almost shouted. And then, she climbed into bed, and waited for her husband to return.

*

It was three in the morning. Joyce climbed out of bed, having not slept a wink. Edward had not returned. Joyce knew he might be gone all night now, something that happened more and more often lately.

She pulled on her wrap and went to the kitchen to make tea. At the stove, she struck a match, waiting for the fire to come on. Nothing. She groaned. They were out of kerosene, again. Well, if she were a better housewife . . .

Entering the living room, she saw that Fred's painting was crooked again. Crazy thing about that picture: it never hung quite right somehow. She reached out to straighten it, and thought suddenly of Ricardo, the Peruvian student who used to visit Dannemora with her. Funny, but she hadn't thought of him, or Plattsburgh State, in a long time. What fun college had been! She'd been special and envied: the only one of the handful of Chinese students on campus who spoke English well, and majored in something other than the Sciences. And there'd been the student senate, and debate team, and the foreign students' association, and the literary arts club. Oh it was silly and sophomoric, and she had outgrown it all by the time she graduated. But the people, and the camaraderie, and that wonderful, wonderful feeling of freedom and strength!

College in America. Another life. No one from that life touched her now. She kept no photographs, wrote no letters. Edward was jealous of souveneirs.

Except for Fred's painting.

Dead flowers against a red plate. Joyce was struck by her present indifference to this painting she'd once proudly displayed in her dorm room. Telling the story to Diana and Michael the other night: how pointless! What would Edward say if . . .

She stopped short in her thoughts. Edward didn't know the whole story about Fred and Dannemora. It wasn't that she deliberately withheld it from him, but he'd fallen asleep the night she reminisced about Fred. Her reminiscences had that effect.

Fred Jefferson had asked to see her when he was scheduled for furlough, and she'd agreed. Although they never actually met because of a change in plans, Joyce knew the only reason he later asked her to take that jewelry out was because he thought she would be willing. After all, she had gone one step further than most of the other visitors, and become a friend, or so he must have reasoned.

Dannemora! Another life!

Joyce lit a cigarette and glanced at the clock. Three thirty. No, Edward wasn't coming back. And she'd have a rough day tomorrow if she stayed up any later. But her mind was racing, with an excitement and vigor she hadn't experienced in ages. What the hell, she thought, as she opened herself a beer. At least she could enjoy her memories, if she couldn't enjoy her husband.

*

Got caught.

The two words echoed in her head as she crossed the road to the bus stop the next morning.

Fred's words. Today, she could not get him out of her mind. When she asked him why he was inside, he had replied,

Unlucky, I guess. Got caught.

Fred Jefferson hadn't been like the other inmates, who were mostly lower income, radical, and black. He was a white, middle class, mainly conservative, college educated man in his early thirties, and a moderately talented painter. It had occurred to her that he had no excuse to be inside.

The bus stopped, and Joyce boarded.

All the way to work, she found herself remembering Dannemora and Fred. Fred had always been a quiet one, who stuck to himself in a corner while the rest took part in noisy debate. How she had loved arguing, especially with the black guys, about Communism, Marxism and the American democratic system. The discussions with the inmates were invariably political. When she first met Fred, however, he talked about himself. A soft spoken and well mannered man, in for drugs or something equally as innocuous. She didn't remember what exactly, but she knew he hadn't been one of the manslaughter or violent crime people.

A memory: One visit, while walking towards the piano, Fred had laid a hand on her shoulder to guide her, and some black guy, another inmate, walking by and saying, hey, watch it, man.

The letters had started after that. Dear Joyce, I paint as many hours as I can in here. It's the only thing that keeps me sane.

Had she been just a little bit in love with Fred? They had corresponded almost a year, but she had stopped after that incident over the jewelry. Fred Jefferson had been a symbol, nothing else. All part of her liberal collegiate image. She shuddered. Was she really so ruthless, and calculating? Oh yes, I visit Dannemora regularly, she could hear herself saying to impress her more naive acquaintances, It's pretty cool rapping with those guys. They're into *international* politics. Even the painting had helped promote the image: how she would guide her friends' remarks — *subterranean* — and then, she would spring upon them the story of Fred Jefferson, Dannemora inmate. Impressed, her friends would study the painting again, certain they detected a "sinister" quality.

How bored bored bored all that pretentious intellectualizing had made her!

The violence of this thought disturbed her. Surely, that was the point of marrying Edward, good old down to earth Edward.

Round about mid afternoon, Edward would wake up — she'd seen him driving in as her bus pulled away — call and apologize for his drunkenness. She would tell him, yes, she'd fed the dogs. He would say . . .

No. That would not do.

The bus pulled into the terminus where she had to make a transfer. As she walked towards the next bus, she remembered herself saying to Fred in an airy, supremely confident tone: no one gets caught because they're unlucky. Dannemora exists because people do what they know they oughtn't do in the first place. And he, agreeing too readily — *yes, yes of course* — continued talking about his paintings.

*

At three in the afternoon, Edward called.

"Joyce? I'm sorry, love."

"I'm sorry."

"What for? It's not your fault I got drunk."

"No?"

"Joyce, come on, girl. No more fighting."

What could she tell him? I'm sorry I'm Chinese and middle class, while you're British working class, but almost better off because this is a colony? I'm sorry I'm ambitious and you're not? I'm sorry I became Mrs. Camden, another symbol in my life of symbols? I'm sorry I got caught? No more fighting, he said, and words equaled fight to him.

"I can't talk now," she said, in the end.

"Oh Joyce. Don't make it difficult, girl."

"We'll talk later."

*

Edward was out when she returned. He had cleaned the house: the floor was cleared of dog hairs and the packing cases of dog food were stacked in a semblance of order. On the table was a vase of fresh flowers.

Joyce sighed. This was home.

She noticed the painting was crooked again. Why didn't the stupid thing hang straight? Edward said it was the wall. She went over to fix it.

This evening, it looked different. Perhaps it was the slant of light on it. She had never noticed the background was bluish gray. Strange how the layers of background colors sloped, making the vase and plate seem to stretch out towards her. A brown vase of dried flowers against a red plate on a black stand. A white border of canvas framed the oblong shaped center. And then, another border, the wood frame, painted olive green. *Oriental*, Fred had described it in a letter. *It reminds me of you. I'll send it to you.*

She glanced at the mail. All bills. To: Mrs. Joyce Camden. A useful name. If Joyce Yu rang up the gas company with a service complaint in Cantonese, no one paid any attention. If Mrs. Camden rang up in English, on the other hand, it was instant service, albeit reluctant, for the British wife. Yu or Camden: a world of difference.

She was sorry, really she was. Edward deserved more than this ambivalent confusion she felt. Being certain was so difficult though. It might take years. Until then, she simply had to make this marriage work. Everyone said it would be over in six months — interracial marriages didn't work in Hong Kong like in America, they whispered. People thought she was bound to go back, because she didn't belong here. Perhaps they had a point, but they were wrong so far.

She had to be sure of something. Edward loved her, that much she knew. Which was why he told her to stick it out here, instead of escaping back to graduate school in America. She'd known they were different from the first. Only now, some of the differences were becoming increasingly harder to bear.

On the wall, the painting, now straight, was enveloped in a fuzzy smear of light.

When Edward came home, she would apologize for picking a fight. They would light up fags, and have beers together at the Sai Kung pub. She would thank him for giving her flowers and tidying up the house.

It struck her suddenly what was wrong about the painting.

The frame. Fred had said it was some old frame he happened to have around.

That was it. She would change the frame. As soon as possible. It needed something darker, more distinctive. Perhaps something Oriental.

THE YELLOW LINE

Everyday he went right up to the tip of that yellow line, never daring to put a toe across. He would be immobilized, his eyes fixed on that line painted on the smooth hard concrete. The yellow line. That sacred yellow line.

He had learnt, parrot-like, the only English he had ever known from that yellow line.

"Please stand behind the yellow line, the train for Chater will soon arrive."

In the shiny caves of Hong Kong's modern new underground, the yellow line separated waiting passengers from the pits of the train tracks. The trains of the Mass Transit Railway moved people from the industrial outbacks of Kwun Tong in Kowloon, to Central, the business district on Hong Kong island. Chater station. Last stop.

He had never been to Chater. In fact, in all of his six years he had never been very far away from his home in Lok Fu low-cost government housing estate. What a day when the Mass

Transit Railway opened! Everyone had rushed to try this new "Underground Iron" — the Cantonese name for the system. The people of Hong Kong had never seen a subway before. At least, not the people of Lok Fu Estate which was his whole world. How he had badgered his mother to take him too! Him too him too, he wanted to ride the underground iron! She had taken him finally, on that great day, into the magic cave of the underground. The mouth was near his home: the huge gaping mouth that swallowed him and his mother. And the funny machine spat out a golden ticket in exchange for a one dollar coin. He had stepped over the yellow line that day, and his mother had screamed at him.

"Stupid child! Do you want to die? Get back over the line unless you want to be killed by the wheels of the train!"

He had jumped back instantly. Never would he dream of disobeying his mother; he did not want to get beaten. The voice in the air spoke to him in Cantonese at that moment, warning him to stay behind the yellow line. Then came the English voice.

"Please stand behind the yellow line. The train for Chater will soon arrive." The droning, monotonous tones echoed around the station.

And then he saw the train! It came racing into the station, faster than anything he had ever seen. The big, shiny iron train.

How he had loved his first ride on the train! It had sped along so quickly. He knew that they were traveling far away. Maybe, even to another country. He had asked his mother whether they were going to China.

"Silly boy. You can't go to China on an underground train."
But his mother had been smiling when she said this to him.

They stopped at the next station, Kowloon Tong, but his
mother would not go out of the station with him. She insisted
that they turn around immediately and take the next train
back. His father would be coming home soon, and she had to
prepare dinner.

"And you're not to tell your father I took you on the
underground iron. He will get very angry if he knows that we
have wasted money like this!" His mother issued the warning
as they rode the train back to Lok Fu.

During all of the next week, he traveled on the underground
iron. Everyday at three o'clock his mother would fall asleep,
having drunk too much again. He would shake his mother,
trying to wake her so that she would take him on the train.
But she would only push him aside and tell him to go away.
The first day, he had found his mother's purse, taken two
dollars, and gone to the underground. His mother would not
miss him, since she was always telling him to go out and play.

In the underground cave, he held his little golden ticket
proudly. He knew how to get to Kowloon Tong! He was not
actually sure where Kowloon Tong was, but at least he did
know how to get there.

On that first day, he arrived at Kowloon Tong and stood at
the exit: the foot of the stairs leading out of the underground
cave. Against a blue, blue sky he saw a tree at the top of the
steps. Did he dare? He was dying to know, to see this place
Kowloon Tong. For a few moments, he hesitated.

And then he ran, for dear life, up those stairs. Outside he saw a wall surrounding a huge playing field. There were also houses, big beautiful houses, not like the tiny flat he and his family lived in. Most of all, he loved the big playing field. If only he could go into that field and run round and round it!

On the second day, he grew bolder and went up to the gate which led into the playing field. He saw some children playing there. They were foreign devil children with golden hair. How rich they must be because they had gold color hair. Everyone knew gold meant lots of money. Like his golden underground iron ticket which cost money. Money was important because his mother was always shouting at his father about money. Last night, he hid under the covers as his mother threw an ashtray at his father for gambling again and losing money. These little boys had golden hair and didn't need any money. They were all happy and laughing. If only he knew how to get money!

The night of the second day he had watched his mother to see if she would notice that he had taken two dollars. She did not seem to miss anything. Good. He could keep riding his train.

"Please stand behind the yellow line . . ."

The third day, he watched excitedly as the train for Chater arrived. Where was Chater? His friend in the next block had told him that Chater was on Hong Kong island. That meant that the train had to go through water. Impossible! He knew that trains could not run under water. He had tried to ask his father who ignored him as usual. On the third day the skies were gray and he thought it might rain. He walked further around Kowloon Tong, to see what this place looked like. If only he knew how close to home he was! He could not know though, for his world had always been just Lok Fu. There was one house he liked very much. It was big and new with a high wall around it. On top of the wall were pieces of colored glass. They looked very pretty. One day, he would live in a house like that too.

The next morning it rained very hard and his mother beat him with a stick because he had been singing too loudly. He knew he would be beaten that morning no matter what he did, because the night before his father had beaten his mother. Whenever that happened he could always expect a beating the next day.

The afternoon of that fourth day, he waited till his mother had fallen asleep and took his two dollars. Into the underground iron he ran, where he was sheltered from the rain. This time he did not go out of the station at Kowloon Tong. Instead, he played hide and seek with himself on all the different staircases of the station. He kept singing and singing; he was so happy because no one told him to stop. He walked along the yellow line and sang the English song about the yellow line. Just like the voice in the air that told passengers to stand behind the yellow line. He wished that it would stop raining so that he could go outside. But the skies remained dark and the rain continued to pour, washing his whole Kowloon Tong a dull gray.

When would his mother notice the missing money? She was always so worried about money, always complaining about money. In the streets in Lok Fu the next day he found a two dollar coin. Someone had dropped it near the bus stop. How wonderful! His ride on the underground iron on the fifth day would be paid for with his findings.

That afternoon, his mother heard him preparing to leave and looked at him sleepily. "Where do you think you're going?" she demanded.

He stood very still, afraid that she would stop him. He knew that she had not finished taking her nap and would fall asleep again soon. If only she would fall asleep quickly! He whispered that he was going out to play.

"Play, play, play! All you ever do is play. You useless, stupid boy. I don't know why you were born. You're too dumb to even go to school you ugly boy, just like your father . . ." Her voice trailed off to incomprehensible mumblings. Soon he heard a little snore, and he knew that she was sound asleep again.

Since he was later than usual on that fifth day, he did not stay in Kowloon Tong very long. He saw a boy with golden hair standing on a board with wheels and speeding along the pavement. He had never seen a skateboard before. What good fun it looked! He wished he could speak English to ask the boy to lend it to him for just a little while. He notice that the train was very crowded on this day. Perhaps it was Sunday, the day many people did not go to work. To him, each day was much like the other.

He wondered why his mother seemed to be watching him very closely the next day. Perhaps she knew that he had been taking money. He did not know what to do. Riding on the train each day had been his greatest joy. That afternoon, while his mother was sleeping, he took enough money for two days. That sixth day he was scared and stared for a long time at the yellow line as the trains passed him by. He put one foot over the yellow line, wondering if anything would happen. Suddenly, the voice in the air shouted at him.

"The little boy in the blue pants, please stand behind the yellow line!" He started and stepped back. He did not think anyone would be watching him.

That night he felt terribly afraid. Somehow he knew that his mother was going to scold him.

"You've been stealing my money, haven't you?" His mother shouted as she approached him menacingly. "Well, haven't you? I know you — you're just like your father. Taking my money and spending it. You're a bad boy!" Her voice was rising to a frenzy now. "I'll teach you not to steal again, I'll beat you!" She hit him hard, again and again and again. He cried out, "Mummy don't beat me. Please don't beat me anymore. I promise I won't steal."

She continued to beat him in a blind fury until the neighbors called the police and she had to stop. When her husband came home, he yelled at her for beating the child, and then he hit her.

He cried himself to sleep that night, knowing that he had only one more ride on the underground iron. His mother told him to stop whimpering.

On the morning of the seventh day, the sun was shining. He began to make a plan for himself. He would not be his mother's ugly boy anymore. He kept very quiet that day, so that his mother would ignore him. No singing, no laughing, no smiles. Nothing to arouse his mother's suspicions. When he knew his mother had fallen asleep, he took his last two dollars and ran to the mouth of the underground cave. Quickly, he had to go quickly very far away to his haven in Kowloon Tong. Only this time, he wouldn't come back.

Kowloon Tong was so lovely on a sunny afternoon. Once again, he saw the boys with the golden hair and his favorite house with the colored pieces of glass cemented into the wall. He went as far as the bus station, where he climbed a tree. It truly was a lovely summer's day, and he was enjoying every minute of it. That last day he completely forgot the time. It would not matter if he never went back because his mother would never find him in faraway Kowloon Tong. All afternoon he played, rejoicing in the fact that his mother would now be awake and wondering where he was. He could sing to himself in Kowloon Tong. No one would stop him. Sometimes people even smiled at him. He knew that they were probably thinking he was a clever little boy because he had traveled so far away from home all by himself on the underground iron train. He would live forever in Kowloon Tong station.

As it grew darker, he crept back into the brightly lit underground cave. Maybe he should go to Chater. He would have liked to visit Chater, to see if the train could really go through water like his friend said. But no, that would be too faraway. He did not know what the distance was, but he knew that there were many stations to Chater.

It was time to go home. He bought his golden one dollar ticket from the funny machine. Proudly, he walked to the train platform. He knew the way. No one had to show him because he was an experienced traveler on the underground iron. And on the concrete platform he could see it: the yellow line, that sacred yellow line.

He went right up to the tip of the yellow line, just as he had done all week.

"Please stand behind the yellow line; the train to Chater will soon arrive."

The voice in the air sang to him first in Cantonese, then in English. Then he saw it: racing out of the tunnel was that fast, shiny underground train, speeding towards him.

In the distance, the motorman did not see the little six-year-old boy who stood so still at the tip of the yellow line among all the other passengers.

The train was coming closer now. He did not move; he hardly dared to breathe. As the train pulled swiftly into the station, he dashed, over that yellow line, into the pits of the train tracks.

THE SIXTIES

ANDREW'S LETTERS

She had been sitting alone for over an hour when Andrew Richards asked her to dance. He was Eurasian. His light brown hair was as straight as hers, and his eyes, though blue, did not sink into hollows like on English faces. He was bigger than his Chinese classmates.

It was a slow number. He held her correctly, the way her father would, with enough distance between them and her right hand balanced in the air. Couples around them were locked in embrace. At thirteen and a half, she had never slow danced with a boy before.

"Chihng mahn neih gwai sing?" His Cantonese was fluent but slightly accented.

She guessed, correctly, that he probably didn't speak it at home. "Would you prefer English?"

"I'd like that." He guided her waist and turned her on the floor. "You don't sound Chinese."

"We speak Indonesian mostly. My parents are *wah kiu.*"

"Oh so you don't take Chinese? Are you taking French?"

"Yes. Are you?"

He nodded. "So we really should get along well then, shouldn't we?"

For the first time that evening, she was glad she was a wallflower because it meant meeting Andrew. She had seen him glance at her earlier that evening. He obviously didn't mind her dark skin the way Chinese boys did.

They danced in silence. Only when the music ended did it dawn on her that, unlike her father, he didn't dance elegantly.

He escorted her back to her seat. A new song came up. "I'll dance if you want, but actually, I'd rather just sit and talk, if you don't mind that is." He looked at her anxiously.

She felt exceedingly grown up when she replied. "Let's. Dancing's a bore. Besides, all they play are the Lettermen, and I don't like them. I like the Platters. Do you?"

In the taxi on the way home, the girls teased her about him.

"You've got a boyfriend now!"

"Did he kiss you?"

"How come you didn't dance?"

"What did you talk about all night?"

"Did you give him your phone number?"

Girls were always like this. They talked about boys as if they weren't real, except as "boyfriends." She hated that word. And they teased because she still hadn't found a boyfriend after three dances that year at the neighboring boys' schools.

She answered haughtily. "We talked about poetry and chess. Maybe we'll meet again, maybe we won't. That isn't what's important. He's very intelligent, and I'd rather talk than dance anyway."

The girls giggled and continued to make remarks. She stared out the window. *Jaahpjung,* they called him. They called her that too behind her back. Tonight, she didn't care. Only why *didn't* Andrew ask for her number, the way boys were supposed to?

The first time he rang, no one else was home.

"How did you get my number?"

"Your surname was the only one in the directory. Good thing you weren't one of the thousands of Chans or Wongs."

She smiled. There had been four Richards when she checked, two on the island, one in the New Territories and one in Kowloon, where he lived. She told him this.

"Are there really?" he asked, but she could tell he was pleased.

They talked for over an hour, mostly about books. He mentioned his younger brother.

"A real Don Juan, just the opposite of me. He gets all the girls."

"I've got a younger sister like that too, with the boys, I mean."

"Horrible, isn't it?"

"Yes," she agreed.

"My brother looks English."

"My sister looks Chinese."

They said together. "Aren't they boring?" And laughed.

He said. "Listen, could I write you? You have pen pals in New Zealand, right?"

She thought a moment. It sounded like fun. "Okay."

"My mother doesn't like me calling up girls."

"So where are you?"

"In a phone booth."

Now, she heard traffic sounds in the background, and wondered why she hadn't noticed earlier.

She asked. "Won't she mind if you get letters from me?"

"Oh no, I always get to the mail before her."

There was a silence.

He said. "I have to go now."

"Thanks for ringing."

She was about to hang up when she heard him say. "Wait. Would you come out with me to a movie sometime? A good one, I mean."

"I guess so."

"Do you have to ask your mother?"

"Oh no." Her response was immediate.

"You're lucky. Well, bye. I'll write."

Afterwards she wondered if that were true. Of course it was! Her mother trusted her, and would never question her judgment. She was honest, not like her sister, who lied.

In his first letter, he wrote about T.S. Eliot. "He's an American, but he left his country for England. Read *Prufrock*. You'll like it." He also began a chess game which, he said, would "be the imperative to continue our correspondence." His letter made her very happy, and she decided to go to the library that very weekend and find *Prufrock*. She also worked out her chess move, and set up a board to watch the progress of their game.

One remark near the end bothered her.

"I'm much older than you, almost sixteen, in fact, although I'm only one form ahead. You're underage. I hope our age difference won't be a problem."

What could she say? Her birth date, at the tail end of the academic year was the reason she was underage. When she'd entered secondary at eleven, she was the youngest in her class. Her mother picked her up from dances then instead of letting her take a taxi with the other girls. Back then, it had mattered when she sat alone in a corner at dance after dance. Once, she couldn't help herself and cried, asking Mum why boys didn't like her, but all Mum said was *don't be ridiculous,* and told her not get so dark in the summer. That time, she knew she was growing up, because she was sure her mother was mistaken: being dark wasn't something she controlled. It had to do with being part Indonesian, like Dad, who was as dark as she was. Couldn't Mum see that?

But that was history. Things were different now.

In her reply to Andrew, she told him she was "mature" for her age. It was true, even if she hadn't begun menstruating while her sister already had, although naturally, she couldn't write about that to him. Never mind. He'd understand. After all, he wasn't like those ignorant boys who only danced with fair skinned Chinese girls.

They wrote daily. Word was out through the grapevine that he had a crush on her. She tried to remain above it but it was difficult, because she felt pleased yet perturbed.

Her girlfriends pestered. "Has he asked you for a date?"

"I've told you," she insisted, "that's not important. He's *not* my boyfriend."

It was her sister who said what her girlfriends didn't.

"I looked up his picture in the yearbook. He's ugly. Why do you want him for a boyfriend?"

"Oh, what do you know?" she retorted. But secretly, she was ashamed to admit that she wished Andrew were better looking, like the boys her sister knew.

Her mother asked. "Who is this A. Richards who keeps writing you letters?"

"His name's Andrew. I met him at a dance."

Mum frowned. "He's not English, is he? You know how the English are. As bad as the Dutch. In Indonesia . . ."

It was a way too long playing broken record, and she cut her off quickly. "Eurasian," and she explained about his strict and unreasonable mother.

"So that's why he writes to you?"

"Yes."

"Well, all right." She sounded dubious. "But don't get carried away. You never know with *jaahpjung*."

"Don't use that word . . ." But her mother disappeared to take care of dinner.

Everyone simply didn't understand. They had strange ideas about other people, but especially about boys and girls together. How was it that Mum, whom she adored, simply wasn't as smart as she used to be? When she was eleven, her mother seemed sensible and grown up, while Dad was too ridiculous for words. Somehow, in the last two years, Dad had become more sensible, and Mum sillier. Also, her sister, who used to be "too wild with boys," seemed to be in her mother's good graces now.

In his last letter, Andrew had asked. "People and things change, and you don't even notice till it happens. Don't you find that so?" His question reassured her. At least Andrew understood.

Things were changing all the time now. Her sister still provoked her, but she didn't need to argue back anymore. She also told her mother less about her life, saving the best parts for Andrew instead.

They really *were* alike. His letters were the best thing that ever happened to her.

It was about three weeks after their correspondence began that she first noticed some differences between them.

In their chess games, he always found the shortest route to eliminating her queen. She thought this odd. "I like removing as many pieces as I can," she wrote him, "and then head for checkmate. Don't you think that's easier?"

"Maybe," he replied, "but the queen's the important prize because she has power. It's the game that counts, not just checkmate."

There were other things. After reading *The Love Song of J Alfred Prufrock,* she thought Eliot wonderful. Andrew was far more critical. He had studied the poem at school, which was probably why he could see faults she couldn't. That was the way it was with school. When it came to Keats, however, she had to disagree.

"How can you say 'Nightingale's' the most 'spectacular' ode? The poet gets drunk, knows beauty, loses it and then plunges into self pity. 'Grecian Urn' is another story. There's balance, harmony, a superb sense of order. It's much more beautiful."

"Perhaps I believe only in the moment, no matter what the consequences might be," he replied. "Call it, if you must, a flaw in my personality."

Yet despite these difference, she knew that Andrew made her think about life in a new way. She liked that. He made her feel clean and whole. After all, no matter how much she loved her family and friends, they wouldn't always be around. Feelings, she knew, would remain.

They had been pen pals for almost two months when he rang a second time. No one was home.

"I can't talk long," he said.

There were all sorts of things she wanted to say, but all she said was, "okay."

"Simon Choi and Joseph Ho have a crush on you."

"They hardly know me."

"They heard you at the inter-school debate yesterday."

"Were you there?"

"Yes."

"Why didn't you come over and say hello?"

"Oh, I had to do something for my Mum. You know how she is."

"Yeah, sure."

There was a pause, like the stillness right before dawn.

He said, abruptly. "Promise me that no matter what

happens, you'll always write me?"

"Oh, I guess so."

"No, you've got to swear."

It puzzled her, but Andrew and she were forever anyway. "I promise."

She thought he sighed.

"Okay, goodbye. Write me."

Their conversation made her uneasy. She didn't believe him. It would have taken no time for him to say hello yesterday.

Time raced by. It was her sister's thirteenth birthday, and she was giving her first mixed party. Mum asked. "Why don't you invite Andrew to your sister's party? You can't just write letters to each other."

"Why not?"

Her sister piped up "Yeah. Tell him to bring his brother. He's cute."

Mum frowned. Her sister scooted off. Her mother seemed determined to "talk."

"It's not normal, writing like this, that's why. Why doesn't he ask you out on a date? Or call you up if he wants to talk?"

"I've told you. His mother's difficult."

"Ah doo. What's the matter with her? Chinese like us not good enough for Chinese like her? Her son's only a *jaahp-jung."*

"Don't use that word!"

"Stop raising your voice. It's just an expression, something all the locals use. You don't know Hong Kong. These *jaahp-jungs* think they're better than Chinese. The ones in Indonesia were like that too. But neither the British nor the Dutch want anything to do with them."

"Andrew's *not* like that."

"Then invite him to the party. Let him bring his brother if he wants. He must meet you sometime. You can't hide behind letters forever."

"We're *not* hiding!"

But her mother had already bustled off to the kitchen, ignoring her outburst.

She invited Andrew in her letter that evening.

"My mother says you can bring your brother. Did I tell you my silly sister thinks he's cute? Younger siblings are absurd, aren't they?"

There, Andrew would understand what she meant. She went to post the letter.

It was still early, and traffic cluttered the streets of Tsimshatsui. How lucky she was to live on the twelfth floor, away from the mess and noise. The post box was a five minute walk from her building. When she reached it, she glanced at the envelope. Kadoorie Avenue. Rich area. Her family wasn't poor, of course, but she'd often thought it would be nice to live in the sort of area Andrew did, where there were trees and low rises, instead of just skyscrapers.

She kissed the letter for good luck and popped it in. On her way home, she thought about how faraway from her Mum was going. Mum still thought in terms of *jaahpjung*, which was pointless. If Andrew were *jaahpjung*, so was she. Indonesian and Chinese. That was a mixture too. Of course, she suddenly thought, the Indonesian blood didn't come from her mother's side at all, did it?

*

Andrew came to the party and presented her a bunch of lilacs. She blushed as she took the flowers. He didn't bring his brother.

They danced once, and talked the rest of the evening. At one point, she asked him, "Why didn't your brother come?"

"He only goes to English parties."

"Silly, isn't that?"

"Yes," he agreed

*

Mum said he was fat but polite. "He doesn't look Chinese, except for his eyes," she added, "and he's not a very good dancer, is he?"

"What does it matter if he isn't?" She was holding the vase filled with his lilacs. Her hands shook and water spilled on the table. "Why do you worry about such stupid things?"

"Lah-ee-lah, look at this mess." Her mother wiped away the water with a cloth. "Don't get so excitable. Andrew's a nice boy, even if he is a *clumsy-lum."*

Normally, her mother could make her laugh with those expressions of hers, but she refused to even smile.

"There's nothing wrong with dancing badly," her mother continued, putting the cloth away. "Not everyone can dance like your father. You mustn't sit at a party all night long. Girls should dance with lots of boys. You'll meet more that way, especially since you're always complaining you never get asked to dance. How do you expect to get asked if you sit with one boy all night?"

"But I don't want to meet my sister's stupid friends!"

"Don't be stuck up. You're too proud, that's your problem. Andrew's not your boyfriend. That's what you keep saying, right? Besides, he hasn't even asked you out."

"No, but . . ."

"Then calm down."

She resolved then and there never to go out with Andrew even if he asked. She did *not* want a boyfriend. Only girls who giggled and acted silly like her sister had "boyfriends." Andrew was better than that. She'd tell him. He'd understand.

The third time he rang, a week after the party, her mother received the phone.

"It's for you, dear. A boy." She smiled conspiratorially.

She wished Mum would go away. Instead, her mother sat in the living room and pretended to sew. Her insides tightened.

Andrew said. "Will you go out with me to a movie on Saturday?"

"No."

"Oh." Then, he added. "It's your mother, isn't it?"

"Yes," she lied.

"But I still can write you, can't I?"

"Yes."

"Okay."

They rang off, and she raced towards her room. Mum's voice intercepted.

"Was that Andrew, dear?"

"Mmmh."

"Did he ask you out?"

"Mmmh."

"Stop mumbling and look at me. Where are you going?"

She kept her back to her mother. "Nowhere. I had to turn him down."

"Why?"

"I wasn't free that day."

Feeling triumphant, she raced into her room. It wasn't until late at night, when no one would hear, that she cried.

Andrew's letters changed after the last phone call. When she read his or wrote back, both acts made her feel different than before. The clean and whole feeling had become tenuous and uncertain. Even after she told Andrew the truth, that her mother had been sitting right there and embarrassed her, she still felt something was missing in their letters.

He reassured her. "It's okay if we don't go out to movies or anywhere else. I like our letters and want to keep writing to you. Mothers make things difficult, don't they? You'll see. It'll be different someday."

She read that paragraph three times, and wondered why his acceptance annoyed her. That night, instead of replying as she usually did, she watched a movie with Mum.

*

Another month passed. Riots broke out on Nathan Road and her sister got stuck in the bus on her way home from school. Her mother shook her head as she listened to the news, saying *"wah doo, ahdoo ahdoo.* This is very bad."

In their letters, Andrew won more chess games than her.

*

After the final rounds of the inter-school debates, Joseph Choi invited her to a party. She looked around to see if Andrew were in the audience, but did not see him. She told Joseph she would think about it.

That evening, she told her mother about the party, adding, "I don't know if I should go. He seems rather boring."

"Now, there you go again, judging everyone. Aren't you grateful he asked you to go?

"No. He doesn't even understand the debates. The only reason he attends . . ."

"Is to see my big sister, the debate team captain," her sister interrupted. "Everyone knows he has a crush on you."

"But he doesn't even know me!"

"Now girls, stop arguing."

Talking to anyone just didn't make sense anymore. She began a letter to Andrew, but stopped after the first paragraph indicating her chess move. Now, even writing to Andrew didn't make sense. What she really wanted to ask him was why did Joseph have to ask her to a party when all she wanted was to sit with Andrew somewhere and talk to him for as long as she could. But she couldn't write that.

She tore up the letter and read "Ode on a Grecian Urn."

Thou foster child of silence and slow time. If only time really were slow! But the days sped by, with school and street riots and debate and parties. Everyone had parties now. Mum would pick out new Butterick and Simplicity patterns to sew dresses for her and her sister. Everyone — her friends, Mum, her sister — seemed to expect she would attend. Even the parties were different. Since her debate team had won its way into the finals, boys *wanted* to dance with her. But they all said the same stupid things, about how clever she must be to lead a winning team, and then wanted to slow dance and touch her with "too many hands."

Andrew didn't mention the debates. Instead, he told her that other boys, not just Joseph Ho and Simon Choi, talked about her. "What does it feel like," he asked, "to be so terribly popular? My chess team won the inter-school tournaments, you know, but no one cares about chess. You don't have to be on stage to play."

Nothing made sense, she thought, as she silently continued to read the ode, except perhaps Keats.

Reaching the end, she closed her text and recited.

"When old age shall this generation waste
Thou shalt remain, in midst of other woe
Than ours, a friend to man, to whom thou say'st,
'Beauty is truth, truth beauty, — that is all
Ye know on earth, and all ye need to know.'"

That clean and whole feeling, that beautiful, joyful feeling. Why had it left? Wasn't that the truth Keats meant? Surely this beauty was not like the nightingale's, fleeting and temporary? Perhaps Andrew was right about the moment. Perhaps there were only moments, nothing else.

She did not write to Andrew for a whole week.

Despite her silence, Andrew neither wrote nor called. It was as if he waited to see what she would do. Well, what did he *expect* her to do? Any other boy . . . Andrew was all wrong and right at the same time.

She called Joseph to tell him she would go to the party. That pleased Mum, who was even more delighted when he came to pick her up. He was, in her mother's words, the perfect escort for a dance. But that was only because Joseph was Chinese, slim and good looking, and planning to be a doctor.

Once before, Mum had asked what Andrew planned to be. When she said she didn't know — they never wrote about such things — Mum said it was very bad for a boy to show so little ambition. This remark troubled her enough to ask him if in fact he did have ambitions, to which he replied, he would rather like to simply write letters to her forever. She didn't tell Mum that.

The party with Joseph was, as she anticipated, boring. All he wanted to do was slow dance, and had nothing to say for himself. He made her feel cold. In bed that night, she tried to imagine how dancing like that with Andrew would feel. Warm and thrilling, she knew, because she had imagined it before, and just a little bit frightening as well.

Another week passed without correspondence. She half expected Mum to say something, but her mother seemed not to notice. Finally, Andrew sent a short note.

"Joseph is your boyfriend now, isn't he? That's what everyone says. Why won't you write me? If you really want him, that's up to you. But you know, don't you, that we belong to each other?" He indicated his chess move, adding, "I've got your queen for sure this time. You promised you'd always write. I love you."

Suddenly, everything made sense again. The clean and

whole feeling flashed through her like a bolt of power. Tonight, she would call Joseph and tell him not to bother calling again. She would also tell him not to say he was her boyfriend because it was untrue. If girls at school asked, she would tell them the same thing.

She laid aside Andrew's letter, meaning to reply later. First, she would run those errands for Mum.

That night, her mother behaved strangely. All through dinner, Mum kept giving her sidelong glances as if there were soot on her nose.

When she headed to her room afterwards, Mum followed, and stood by the door when she sat down at her desk.

Finally, she said. "I want to write a letter," hoping that would make her go away.

"Is it to Andrew, dear?"

"Yes."

Her mother held up a sheet of paper. "Is this the letter you're replying to?"

She reached quickly under the desk into the slot where she kept Andrew's letters. They were gone.

"I read the letter," said her mother, "and some of the others as well once I realized what was going on. Now, don't get upset. I only did it for your own good."

For once, she simply didn't know what to say.

Mum came close and sat beside her. She gently rearranged her hair, the way she would when she was a child. "Poor girl," she said softly.

But she hardly heard her. All her thoughts converged at one

point: *Mum had read Andrew's letters!*

"You don't understand, do you, what Andrew wants? He wants to sleep with you, to have sex with you. And he's trying to keep you away from other boys because he's jealous. These *jaahpjung* are all the same. And what horrible things he's been saying about your friends. This is a mean boy. Do you really want him for a boyfriend?"

"But," she whispered, "he's *not* my boyfriend."

"And these dirty innuendoes in his letters," continued her mother, as if she hadn't heard. "What does he mean by 'wild ecstasy' and 'breathing human passion' and 'getting your queen' and other such words? Doesn't he think you're a virgin? Does he expect you to be like the English girls, who have sex when they're teenagers, or those Chinese girls who go with English boys? The wild ones?"

It was hard to breathe. "Poetry, chess," she explained. "He's writing about poetry and chess. He doesn't think such awful things about me. He can't."

Mum stroked her hair. "Oh dear, I warned you not to get carried away. You just don't understand boys, or the *jaahp-juhng*. Don't you know the girls become prostitutes?" She hushed the last word, as if the quiet could erase its sting. " You know what those are, don't you? And just think," she went on, "if you were to marry a boy like that when you grew up and had a little girl, she would be a *jaahpjuhng* too. Is that what you want? You're lucky that a nice boy like Joseph Ho will pay attention to you. I wouldn't be surprised if Andrew's told the boys at school that he slept with you."

"But we haven't done anything like that!"

"I know, dear. But Andrew has too much imagination, and he could twist your words all out of shape. Now, I know you've probably not written anything bad in your letters. All Mum's daughters are good. But don't you see, if you reply to this letter, and say you love him — now I know you may not mean to do that, but just suppose if — then Andrew could go around telling everyone you're his lover. And you know what people would think."

"But he wouldn't do that. Andrew . . ."

She meant to say Andrew loved her, but her voice faltered. How hopeless everything felt! The clean and whole feeling would vanish, and who knows when it would come back? Her mother droned on.

One thought echoed: *Mum was wrong!*

There was only one thing to do.

She simply stopped listening.

At that moment, the space inside her where she trusted her mother unconditionally, closed, forever.

"And I want you to stop writing to him," Mum was saying. "You must promise me never to write again, and never to say you love him. I know you thought he was a nice boy, but I'm your mother and a better judge. You must promise me."

She could not make such a promise! She refused to reply.

Her mother was undaunted. "I won't forbid you, because you're old enough to be responsible. Please promise me, and we'll never talk about this again."

The little space had become a safe into which all Andrew's letters would be hidden, at least until she could open it again. She looked at the kindly Mum face she had once depended on, and saw a debate opponent. Quickly, she had to think quickly. "Can I write just one letter to tell him I won't be writing anymore? Just a short one?"

Her mother considered. "Yes," she said. "That would be a sensible thing to do. And so that you know how much I trust you, I won't even ask to read it."

"Can I have the rest of the letters back?"

"I've burned them, dear. You see, it's best not to dwell on these things. Mum does have more experience than you so don't be too angry."

Her mother left her then to "think about things." She did not write to Andrew. Late that night, when the whole family was asleep, she stood on the verandah and stared at the dark. No tears came. They had frozen inside her. At two, she went to bed and lay awake till morning returned.

*

She overheard Mum telling her sister. "Your sister has had a nasty shock. You must promise to be nice to her. You're lucky because you're prettier than she is, but that means you should learn to help. Tell her Joseph is a nice boyfriend, a handsome one, and flatter her and say she's pretty. That'll make her feel better. Can you do that?"

And she heard her sister reply, in the same awed tones she herself had used when all those times before, Mum asked for *her* help with her "wild" sister. "Yes, Mum, I promise."

*

Her last letter to Andrew was short.

"I can't write anymore. My mother read your letters, and made me promise not to write and not to say I love you.

"I promised I wouldn't write.

"But you know we'll be writing forever, don't you?

"Nothing makes sense right now, but that's just the way things are. You were right. It will be different someday.

"Next week, I'll be fourteen. Time's going to move awfully slowly for awhile.

"By the way, this last time you took my queen, you'll be able to place me in check with just one more move.

"Goodbye Andrew. Thank you for your letters."

CHUNG KING MANSION
from *Chinese Walls*

On my ninth birthday, my mother sits me down in front of her dressing table mirror and brushes my hair. She tells me a story of Indonesia, the country of her birth.

"Before the war when I was still a little girl, no bigger than you are today, Ai-Lin, my parents had a big house in Tjilatjap. My brothers took me down to the beach and told me to be careful of the crocodiles." She stops and laughs. "Maybe one day you will meet your uncles. They were funny, naughty boys, full of energy and life."

I try to imagine this big country Indonesia where my mother was a girl and rode horses on the beach. My mother speaks to me only in English nowadays, a funny, musical accent that's a bit like Chinese and a bit like Indonesian. She used to speak Indonesian to me, and even Mandarin, but stopped because Dad wants all the children to speak good English like him.

From the window of my parents' bedroom, I can see clear

across the harbor to Hong Kong side. It's Saturday morning. I like it when my birthday falls on a weekend and I don't have to go to school.

My mother continues. "My daddy was a very rich man, one of the richest in Tjilatjap. He used to say that the reason he was rich was because he worked hard, and because he was Chinese. Which is why, Ai-Lin, you must always be proud of being a Chinese no matter where you are. Because Chinese people are smart and successful, and don't ever forget that."

Yesterday, my brother Philip got slapped by Mum because he said Chinese people were dirty and afraid of the British, and that Hong Kong would always be a colony, and why couldn't the Chinese be like the Indonesians who fought for their independence against the Dutch.

My mother brushes harder and faster now.

"My daddy was important as well as rich. In Tjilatjap, he was one of the few men that the Dutch administrator would consult on local matters. Your grandfather was never afraid of the Dutch, like some of the other Chinese, or the Indonesians. He was a tall man, and stood tall. He knew what was right."

In the mirror, I see my mother's eyes shining. I like to see her smile because then she is the most beautiful woman in the world. My father is away in Indonesia today, on an important business trip. But he left me a new dress as my birthday present, and Mum gave me an extra kiss which she said was from Dad.

And then, my mother's hand slackens, and she holds my long hair in both her hands. "I was so happy in Indonesia," she says. "One day, I'll go back there for good."

I hang up my new dress and get ready to go to the comic book stand. Paul and Philip have both given me money for my birthday and told me to choose my own comics. I want to buy the new Supergirl. Philip asks why I don't wear my new dress and I tell him, quite sternly since I think he ought to know better, that it would be silly to wear such a nice dress just to go down the street. Philip laughs and says I'm such a prim and proper little lady, and then tickles me until I laugh and cry at the same time. Paul tells Philip to leave me alone.

I take the back lifts down my building because I want to go out the side entrance through the Ambassador Hotel arcade. Nathan Road is already quite busy, even though it's only ten o'clock. My mother doesn't like living in Tsimshatsui; she says this area is too noisy and crowded and wants my father to buy a house in Kowloon Tong or Yau Yat Chuen where there are trees and real houses. But I like Tsimshatsui and our flat which has two floors and an interior connecting staircase. From our verandah on the seventeenth floor, I can watch the Kowloon-Canton railway trains pull into the station, and the grey U.S. battleships dock in the harbor. The sweep of the island's hills are like a picture frame for the buildings dotting the hillside and the waterfront. At night, the neon lights go on. My favorite is the one on top of the low building in the middle with the three red Japanese characters which Dad says is an advertisement for monosodium glutimate. It isn't lonely in Tsimshatsui, or quiet and scary.

The comic book stand is down a side street a few streets away from my building. I go past Chung King Mansion's dingy, cavernous mouth. Two American sailors are going into the building. Their white uniforms gleam like the teeth on the toothpaste commercial on TV. Aren't they afraid of getting their uniforms dirty in there?

I find the new Supergirl issue I want, and buy an extra Batman comic for Philip. Philip pretends he's too old for comics — he's only thirteen — but I've seen him reading them when he thought no one was looking. Boys are so silly, even big boys like my brothers.

The comics tucked under my arm, I run back along Nathan Road towards Middle Road where my building is. As I near Chung King Mansion, I slow down. Coming down the steps of that building is the strangest looking person. She has orange hair, and wears a short cheongsam with a stiff high collar and very high heels. There's something unreal about her, like she's a doll that's come to life. I watch her slow, uncertain progress down the steps, as if she hasn't learnt how to walk in heels. My mother says it's very important for a lady to know how to walk properly in high heels, with her legs straight, taking firm but graceful steps. When I grow up I will learn how to walk correctly in heels.

But this woman on the steps obviously hasn't learnt.

"Paul," I ask that evening, "have you ever been inside Chung King Mansion?"

My big brother looks up from his school books and his glasses slide down his nose. "Why are you asking?"

"Well, have you?" I know if I persist, he will eventually tell me. Paul is the best brother in the world.

He pushes up his glasses. "Yes."

"Is it dangerous in there?"

"Sometimes. Now can I finish my homework?"

I think about this a moment and then give him a kiss on the cheek, which is the way I thank him, and go upstairs to find Philip.

Philip is at the piano in the bedroom of course, which is where he always is instead of doing his homework. He doesn't like to be bothered when he's practising, but I can tell that he's just fooling around and not really playing. So I sit on the bench next to him.

"How come some Chinese women have orange hair?"

He stops playing and looks at me. "Are you dreaming?"

"You know, like the ladies outside Chung King Mansion."

"Oh them." My brother looks embarrassed. "They want to look Eurasian."

"But why?"

Philip makes an impatient face and I can see he doesn't want to tell me. My best friend Helena Choy is Eurasian, but she has black hair like me and doesn't look one bit like the Chung King ladies at all.

My mother's voice sails up from the living room. "Philip, can you go get my prescription?"

"Can't Paul go?"

"He's doing his homework, which is more than you're doing. Now go."

I tug my brother's arm. "Can I go too?"

Philip grabs the back of my neck. "Okay, come along."

My mother frowns a little when she sees me with Philip at

the door. She always says that young girls shouldn't go out too late, especially when the sailors are out. I've never been quite sure what she means by that, but whenever I've asked, she replies that I'll find out when I've grown up. But she lets me go, because it's my birthday, and warns Philip, "Don't you two dilly dally."

I dance alongside Philip, clutching his arm. We go down in the front lifts and walk out onto Middle Road. Across the road, I see some older kids going into the bowling alley. Paul says bowling isn't a real sport, and a waste of money. But then, he thinks everything is a waste of money. I'm going into the bowling alley someday, when I'm older.

"Want to go over the hump?" Philip asks and I nod excitedly. The "hump" is the path next to the Royal Observatory that lets us out right in the middle of Mody Road. My mother calls it the hump because it curves uphill and down again like the hump on a camel's back. Dad says that silly. But I like the name because it's our family's private name for it, which somehow makes the path our own secret, special way.

At the end of the hump, there are low buildings, only three or four storeys high, on a small *cul-de-sac*. Its mouth is flanked by two huge trees, which my mother says have been there forever. "Concrete jungles are built around the real jungle," she says. "In Indonesia, there's too much foliage and jungle for the buildings. There, unlike Hong Kong, nature is stronger than the vain egos of men." My mother says strange things sometimes. She doesn't like buildings. I like the low buildings, but the trees and the hill of the Royal Observatory block their view. Not like my building, with its wonderful wide open view of the Hong Kong harbor, which Dad says is one of the most scenic harbors in the world, matched only by San Francisco and Rio de Janeiro. I'm going to both those harbors when I grow up to see for myself.

At the pharmacy, the store clerk says to me in Cantonese, *"Muihmui yuht laih yuht dai aah."* Little sister is getting bigger and bigger. He has a nice smile. Philip takes the wrapped package of medicine. "It's her birthday," he says pointing to me, and the man tugs my ponytail and asks how old I am and I tell him. The man speaks funny Cantonese, and Mum says that's because he's from Fukien, like us. I thought we were from Indonesia but Mum says our family was originally from Fukien, which doesn't make much sense to me. But I don't speak funny Cantonese, and neither do my brothers. It's only our parents who do.

"Want to go home the long way?" Philip asks, and I nod. Mum would have gone over the hump, because it's faster. She's always in a hurry.

The long way is up Mody Road towards Nathan Road, and back to Middle Road. We make a circle. At the junction of Nathan and Mody, Tsimshatsui comes alive like a huge electric circus.

It's sailor night. I see hordes of them all over the place. There was a new battleship this morning docked in the middle of the harbor, flying a Stars and Stripes. My mother says it has to do with the war and R&R. I don't know what she means. I thought the war she always talks about with the Japanese in Indonesia was over before I was born.

"Sailors walk funny," Philip whispers to me as we pass a group of them. "That's because their pants are too tight and their bell bottoms flap around under their knees."

"They look like ducks," I say, and Philip starts making silly quacking noises.

As we near Chung King Mansion, I see her again. Orange hair, orange nails, wearing a shiny, satiny short cheongsam that fits her so tightly I think it will burst. She's standing at the top of the stairs like a princess waiting to go to the ball. Her voice is bright and cheerful as she laughs and talks with the other ladies. "It's her," I tell Philip, trying to point discreetly. But by the time he pays attention to me and looks, she's disappeared back into the building.

That night, I dream about my orange lady. She is standing at the foot of the stairs wearing an orange gown like Cinderella's fairy godmother in my picture book. *"Muihmui, yahp laih."* Little sister, come in. I start to follow her, but a group of American sailors rush past and knock me down. Her hollow laugh, like the voice of a ghost, floats into the air as she drifts back into the darkness of Chung King Mansion.

I've been nine almost a whole week now and I think I like being nine. I feel like I'm a lot closer to being grown up than when I was eight. My mother tells me things all the time now that Dad's away a lot. She cries when Dad's away. She says men are not to be trusted, because they have too much pride and have to feel important. Also, men don't understand love. In life, she says, these are things I must never forget.

She's right. Those American sailors who've been roaming the streets of Tsimshatsui all week are always talking loudly about love. They let lots of girls run after them, because they're proud. I know. I've seen them. Everyone knows you don't shout about love all over the place. That's what Mum says.

It's Friday evening and Mum needs her medicine again. She always gets sick when she talks too much. I've told her I'll go to the pharmacy because both the boys are still out. At first, she doesn't want to allow me, but in the end she lets me because I'm grown up and responsible enough now to go quickly there and back, she says.

I go past Chung King Mansion and look for my orange lady. I haven't told Mum about her because Mum's not well and doesn't have time to listen to my silly stories.

She isn't there either on my way out or on my way back. As usual, there are a group of ladies in brightly colored cheongsams around.

At dinner, I ask, "Why are there so many ladies around the entrance to Chung King Mansion?"

Philip chortles. "They're not exactly 'ladies' Ai-Lin."

"Do you know any of them?"

This time, Paul suppresses a laugh. "He better not."

Suddenly, my mother bangs her spoon hard. "You boys are getting more like your father every day. There's nothing to laugh at!"

"We were only . . ." begins Paul in a conciliatory tone.

"Be quiet!"

No one speaks for a few minutes. I don't understand why Mum is so upset. And I still didn't get an answer to my question. So I try again. "But who are they, those ladies?"

Mum raises her voice. "That's enough questions from you. These things don't concern you until you're grown up!"

I bend my head over my dinner and don't say another word. It seems I'm only grown up when my mother says so.

Mum needs the clasp on her pearl brooch fixed.

To get to Linda Yue's jewellery shop, I cross Nathan Road and go down Peking Road past the topless bar with pictures of half naked women that Philip snickers at.

Mrs. Yue is wearing a cheongsam, which is all she ever wears. Her shop is fragrant with flowers and perfume.

"Good girl," she says, when I hand her the brooch. "Your mama must trust you a lot if she lets you go out alone."

Mrs. Yue speaks funny Cantonese too, like almost everyone my parents know or do business with. She and her husband are Shanghainese, and are members of the Jockey Club, which is how we know them. Their daughter is in my class. Mum buys all her jewellery from her because of our connection. Everything grown up seems to be connected.

"Here," she hands me a bunch of violets. "Bring to your mother," she says in English.

"Thank you aunty," I reply. I know what Mum will do. She'll make a face and say — *what does she give me these cheap flowers for?* — so I'll keep them. I like these small violet bouquets with their deep green circular leaf base. Sometimes, when I go to the flower market with Mum, the man she buys from gives me a bunch. My mother doesn't like violets. She says they're what men give to vulgar women at the theatre in

Europe and sugar daddies give to girls. I'm not sure what she means by that because I've never been to Europe.

Outside the shop, I see the junks in the distance along Canton Road waterfront. Paul is the only one who's allowed to go all the way down to Canton Road, because my parents say it's dangerous there. I sneaked down there once with Philip, but couldn't see what the big deal was about. It was just an ordinary street, kind of dirty, but with *daaih paaih dong*, hawker food stalls. Philip bought me a bamboo stick with fish balls and pig skin. It was yummy, but Mum would have punished us if she'd known.

I pass the bar and see my orange lady. She's talking to some of the bargirls. Dad calls them taxi girls, because he says sailors hail them like a taxi which sounds funny to me. I don't think my orange lady is really their friend. She looks rather special and different. For one thing, I never see her smoking a cigarette, which all the other girls seem to do. And she seems to be important — even now in the afternoon when there are hardly any sailors around, she is talking, laughing, in the center of everything.

"Philip, what's a prostitute?"

My brother stares at me as if I'm crazy. "Where did you learn that word? Paul, did you hear what she asked?"

"Mum said it to Dad last night when they were talking loudly in their bedroom. I heard them."

Sometimes, I wish I could use a dictionary properly, but it's too hard looking up words I can't spell. I can see Philip is not going to tell me. He gets this look whenever he wants to play big brother, and cracks his knuckles. Paul is a different story. Even though Paul's the really good brother who knows when to stop fooling around, he doesn't put on the "you're too young for that" act like Philip sometimes does. I guess that's because Paul's older and really is grown up.

Paul responds. "They're women who make a life from being with men."

I think about this a moment. "You mean like Mum?"

Philip cracks up laughing and yanks my ponytail. "Sometimes, Ai-Lin, you're just too hilarious."

Paul is smiling as he replies. "No, not exactly. They're not married women. Many of them don't have much money and so they pretend to be a girlfriend to men who pay them."

"So they're like actresses?"

"Sort of."

This explanation doesn't fully satisfy me, but at least now I know the meaning of the word. I give Paul a kiss and leave him to his school books.

That night, I hear my parents talking very loudly again. Dad has only been home a few days. The last time he went away and came back, I remember my parents talking loudly like this. Sometimes, I wish we lived in a big house, which Mum wants also, then I could have my own room and my brothers could each have their rooms and so could Dad and Mum. But as Dad always says, this is Hong Kong, not Indonesia, and we're lucky to have as big a flat as we do. I'm never quite sure what he means by that, since I've never been to Indonesia.

In my dream, the orange lady has her back to me. Her nails are very long and orange. I go up to her, to ask if she'll be my friend. When she turns around, her face is pale and heavily made up. It's my mother's face, but she stares at me as if I'm a stranger. I scream and run away.

The dream startles me into wakefulness. I can't go back to sleep so I go quietly downstairs and step out on the balcony. It's around four in the morning. Only a few lights dot the hills of Hong Kong island. Everything is calm and peaceful, unlike my dream.

Singing voices rise from the streets below. I can't quite see them, because it's still dark, but I can tell there are two sailors singing and walking along Nathan Road next to the Peninsula Hotel. Their voices ring out clearly. They're drunk. As Mum says, men sing when they're drunk.

I suddenly hate all U.S. sailors. They don't belong here, making so much noise in the middle of the night.

The day my mother fires Ah Siu the cook, two new aircraft carriers dock right in the middle of the harbor. It's a Saturday.

"She dared to raise her voice to me!" Mum repeats several times that afternoon. "She dared!"

I watch Ah Siu pack her things. She lives in a small room with no window next to the kitchen. I don't want her to go. She always makes me lunch when I come home from school, and sneaks special treats or snacks to me while I'm doing homework. She also helps me with my Chinese lessons, which are really difficult. I can't imagine my afternoons without her, when my mother is usually lying down because she's ill or goes out shopping. My brothers both go to full day school now, so there's often only Ah Siu and me at home most afternoons.

Paul says Ah Siu is much too rude to Mum, and should be asked to leave. Philip doesn't care because he doesn't like to eat and never pays attention to her.

Ah Siu leaves quietly, shortly after lunch. I wonder where she'll go. I have no idea where she lives. She told me once that she had a little girl, the same age as me. When I asked if I could play with her, she replied that her daughter was in China. It seems like Ah Siu has always been with us. Dad says it's fine to have a cook since Mum can't cook, but that looking after us is Mum's job, which is why he won't let Mum hire an *amah* to look after me, according to Philip. Philip says I'm the only baby who still needs looking after.

I feel sad seeing her go. It's not fair. The only reason Mum gets upset is because she doesn't understand Mum's funny Cantonese. Ah Siu always understands when I talk to her. But Mum speaks Mandarin — and even then, Dad says she speaks peculiar Mandarin — so she doesn't say her words right in Cantonese. Naturally, Ah Siu doesn't know what she's saying.

Mum spends the afternoon on the phone with friends from church and the Jockey Club telling them about Ah Siu and what a headache she'll have looking for another cook. After that, she lies down for an hour or so because she does have a headache.

I cry in my room, but no one pays attention to me.

That evening, Dad announces we're going out to eat Shantung chicken at Far East Restaurant to celebrate Ah Siu's departure.

I put on my new red dress which Dad hasn't seen me wearing yet, and he says I'm beginning to look more grown up all the time. This makes me happier than I've been all day. Mum is wearing make up and has drawn her eyebrows so they arch. Dad says she looks fierce like an Empress dowager which makes everyone laugh, even Mum.

We all go over the hump to Far East restaurant which is on Kimberly Street, a back street that doesn't join any of the main roads. The walk takes about fifteen minutes. It's not that dark yet because it's only seven o'clock and lots of shops are still open. I love walking the back streets which are less crowded than Nathan Road. Some of the shopkeepers who recognize us say hello. Paul and I used to roller skate together around these streets. He'd pull me along so that we'd go faster and shout, "hey we're off to Never Never Land!" But Paul doesn't have time to roller skate anymore now that he's getting closer to Form 5 and School Cert, which everyone knows is the most important exam in the world.

"Hsu sang, Hsu tai, hao jiu bu jian! Mr. and Mrs. Hsu, long time no see!"* Mr. Huang, the owner of Far East restaurant greets my parents. My father chats with Mr. Huang. I don't understand much of what he's saying because it's all in Mandarin.

Philip whispers *shu shu sha sha* noises in my ear, which is sort of what Mandarin sounds like, making me giggle.

I know the whole menu by heart, because we hardly ever order anything different. Shantung chicken, pieces of cold chicken which is dipped in a soy garlic sauce; crispy pepper leaves and fried bamboo shoots that look like pieces of fish;

hot steamed shrimps, without the shells; Hunan ham with long leaves of Chinese cabbage in a white sauce; pan fried pork dumplings. The best part though are the white loaves of steamed bread — silver thread bread — which have the soft, thin shreds of bread inside a spongy crust. Paul takes the end and scoops out the shreds which I eat, and fills his cone with shrimp. I love the bread because it means no rice. Rice is so boring Cantonese.

I love eating at restaurants with my family. I get to stay out late and see the streets of Tsimshatsui at night. My brothers don't fight with each other, and Mum doesn't yell at any of us. Dad talks loudly like he always does, but in noisy Chinese restaurants this seems okay somehow, not like at home. Besides, at restaurants, Mum laughs at what Dad says but at home she doesn't. I especially like Far East, because here, Mr. Huang always comes to our table and chats with my father, and sometimes he even pours Dad a glass of brandy which we don't have to pay for.

Mr. Huang comes by tonight and looks across the table at me. *"Hsu xiao jie,"* he begins in his funny Cantonese, "what class are you in now?"

"Primary 4."

"Wa, clever girl, at Maryknoll, right?" He addresses my mother.

She smiles in acknowledgement. My mother is very proud that I'm at Maryknoll, and the boys at La Salle. This is because of her excellent connections with the Catholic Church. I know this is important, because, as she often reminds me, I failed the Chinese entrance exam into Primary 1, and it was only her connections that got me into a good school like Maryknoll.

Mr. Huang smiles a strange smile at me. "They say Maryknoll is full of ghosts. Japanese ghosts."

Dad laughs. "Yes, Ai Lin's always coming home with ghost stories."

I feel my face turning red. I wish Dad wouldn't tell people the silly things I say. Philip is snickering - he knows how scared I get. Once, he put a rubber hand covered with red paint on my bed after I told him the story about the nun's hand hidden under the path in our school from the war with the Japanese. I screamed and ran to Paul who showed me it was just a joke. But I dreamt about it for days afterwards.

"Anyway, enjoy your dinner," Mr. Huang says.

Sometimes, I don't like being the baby in the family.

The night air is cool after dinner, and Mum makes me put on a light cardigan. I don't like it because it covers up my pretty dress, but I do what she says. We walk home along Nathan Road. It's ten o'clock and quite a few people are still about. The moon tonight is as bright as the street lamps.

Sailors mill around the streets, like ants surrounding a dead cockroach on our verandah, looking and leaving and returning again. The sailors don't seem to be going anywhere in particular. But they're there, always there. Like ghosts who must come back to haunt us here on earth.

Outside Chung King Mansion, a flock of women laugh and talk with the sailors. I peer at the women, looking for my orange lady. She's there on the steps, talking and laughing as loudly as the rest. There's something strangely magical about her tonight, like a costumed actress on stage who appears and disappears, declaiming lines to her audience on Nathan Road. She is not a beautiful woman. Her face is chalk white with powder, and her orange hair is a blackish coppery color, like an orange on the market fruit stand that has been scarred and bruised and not fit for sale, as Mum would say. I walk as near to the steps of the building as I dare, to get a closer look at her. And then, I hear Mum's voice, telling me to get away. My mother's face is wrinkled with disgust, and I know she does not like these women.

On Monday, during recess at school, I walk down the path paved with large flat rocks and stop at the black stone halfway between the tower and the covered playground. Under this stone, my friend Helena told me, is the hand of the nun who wouldn't let the Japanese soldier touch her. Helena knows all the ghost stories. I close my eyes and try to imagine Japanese soldiers swarming around the grounds of my school. Instead, I see American sailors in white uniforms surrounding my orange Chung King Mansion lady.

I've been nine for a whole month now, and I think I'd rather be ten. Philip says that until there are two digits in my age, I'm not really grown up yet. This summer during the holidays, Mum says I have to take more private lessons in Chinese, because I've had red marks twice in my report card this year. Miss Yeung, my teacher, told Mum that I would either have to stay back a year to improve my Chinese, or join the English study group next year. Mum was so upset at Miss Yeung that she complained to the principal.

"She dared to say we weren't really Chinese, so it wasn't important for Ai-Lin to learn Chinese! Who does she think she is?" I hear Mum shout at Dad that night. Dad is packing for a business trip to Japan and tells Mum to stop shouting.

"This is all your fault. You should help the children with their homework," she continues. "How do you expect them to learn if you don't help them? You know I can't because my Chinese isn't good enough. I can't help it. My father had to send me to Dutch school because of his connection to the Dutch."

I pull the blankets over my ears. None of this makes sense to me. I've tried hard in Chinese, but it's even harder now that Ah Siu's gone and no one speaks Cantonese to me anymore. My Eurasian friend Helena speaks English. She's lucky. Her mother's Portuguese and doesn't make her study Chinese. Paul used to help me, but Mum made him stop because he had too much homework of his own to do. Philip can't help. He's taking French now in secondary school and says Mum's ridiculous and won't listen to her at all. Philip could help me if he tried. He could have passed Chinese if he wanted to. He understands everything that's said to him because, as Mum says, he has a musical ear. And I know he can read, because I've caught him reading the Chinese paper Dad gets when he thinks no one's watching. But he simply won't study because he's defiant — Mum says Philip's character is bad, and that he will defy everyone to his grave.

Under my blanket, things always feel safer, less scary. It's also easier to think under here when I can block out the noise that doesn't make sense. I know I don't want to study Chinese all summer, but Mum made an agreement with the principal that I wouldn't have to stay back a year if I could pass an extra Chinese exam at the end of the summer.

I've got to do something. Paul says the only way to face the difficult things of life is to persevere. But he's smart, and much more grown up than me. It's easy for him. I try and try but it doesn't do any good just trying.

Tomorrow, when Dad flies off, I'm going to run away from home. I'll pack the B.O.A.C. bag Dad gave me with my latest Supergirl comic, my new red dress and some clean socks and underwear. Oh, and my toothbrush. I don't think I'll need anything else.

The next day Mum has a headache again. She has a headache every weekend and also when Dad goes away. She's so predictable.

I'm going to get her prescription, but I'm not coming back. I don't care if she suffers from her headache. Maybe if I run away she won't make me do all these things I can't do. Maybe then she'll miss me and be sorry and won't shout at me anymore if I come back. Of course, maybe I won't ever come back.

Downstairs in the hallway of our building, I go to the little shop way at the back next to lift number 5 to buy myself a vitasoy drink which I drink right there. Mum doesn't let me drink vitasoy; she makes me drink milk instead which has calcium, but I don't like the taste of milk. The fat man who minds the shop asks me where I'm going this afternoon with my airline bag. I tell him I'm going to visit my friend. When he asks where my friend lives, I say Chung King Mansion.

"So go through this way." He points to a back alley and path I've never seen before.

"Where does that go?"

"*Heihyah,* here you say you're going to Chung King Mansion and you don't even know the way?"

I don't like the fat man. He wears a filthy singlet and shorts, no shirt, and rubber thongs. I don't think he's very clean. His hands are grimy and his long pinky nail is yellowish black.

"Of course I know the way. I just want to be sure, that's all."

He chuckles and takes the empty soy drink bottle I hand back to him. "*Siujeih* is clever, aren't you?"

So because I don't want him to think I didn't know the way, I go through the opening at the back of the shop and through the dark alley. And there I am, in Chung King Mansion.

It's the middle of the afternoon, and a number of people are in the main foyer. It looks like an ordinary building to me, and I wonder now why my mother always makes such a fuss about it. There are some Indian tailors, like the ones in the arcade of the Ambassador Hotel which I pass by often. I see lifts which look like the ones in our building.

And then, I see her again, waiting for the lift.

She looks different somehow. Her orange hair isn't quite as orange anymore, and the black roots are prominent. She has no makeup on, and she's wearing ordinary clothes, a pair of cotton slacks and a blouse. But it's definitely my orange lady. I recognize her.

I walk up close, and realize she's only a little taller than me. She isn't smiling and laughing. In her hand is a cloth net bag filled with vegetables and meat wrapped in newspaper. She looks just like Ah Siu when she's come home from the market.

The lift arrives and she holds open the door after she goes in.

"Hey little sister, are you coming or not? I'm not holding this door all day."

It dawns on me that she's talking to me. I shake my head and quickly walk away. She makes an impatient noise.

At the entrance of Chung King Mansion, I stop at the top of the stairs and look at the bustle of Nathan Road. There are sailors coming up the steps. I don't know why, but I begin to cry. My orange lady scared me. Her ordinary speaking voice isn't melodious and sweet as I've always imagined, but rather rough and deep, like the hawker woman at the market. But what I didn't expect at all is that she is not really much older than me, like one of the girls in the upper classes at school. She isn't the grown up lady I thought she was. She isn't grown up at all.

I wipe my eyes with the back of my hand and walk down the steps.

That evening, I don't run away after all and return home instead with my mother's prescription.

For months afterwards, I avoid passing Chung King Mansion, especially in the evenings.

I've been nine a whole summer now. Tomorrow, school

starts again. I only just managed to pass the extra Chinese exam, because Miss Yeung gave me private lessons all summer and Paul had time to help me. This school year, my mother says I have to improve my arithmetic which also isn't very good.

This summer, there were more battleships on the harbor than I can ever remember seeing. Dad says the Americans have to continue the war in Vietnam, and that Tsimshatsui is turning into a red light district because of it. Mum says Tsimshatsui always was a red light district only slightly better than Wanchai and if my father had any sense he'd buy our family a house in Kowloon Tong. When I ask my brothers to explain what my parents mean, Philip tells me to hang a red light outside Mum's door to really make her mad. And Paul says war is sad and horrible, but confirms that the Japanese really have nothing to do with this one. None of this makes any sense to me.

This afternoon, Mum has a headache because there's been so much to do before my brothers and I start school.

In the evening, I see my orange lady again. She is all orange, her hair dyed to match her orange dress and nails. I hang around in the streets much longer than I'm supposed to and watch her perform. She is smiling, laughing, talking to sailors. After a little while, she takes one sailor by the arm and leads him into the building. Even though I can't see her face, I'm sure she's not smiling anymore.

I walk home slowly, past Chung King Mansion, my mother's prescription in my hand.

DEMOCRACY
for Abbe Wong Mee Chun

That Thursday of the vote, Patricia Chow awoke feeling queasy. Had the sixteen-year old been more honest, she would have known her illness for what it was: a distraction. The truth of her discomfort was the Girl Guides meeting that afternoon, and the election she might win, beating Maria for the position of the 19th Kowloon's first ever Company Leader.

At breakfast, her father said. "There's going to be trouble today." On the radio, news of the unrest dominated. It was early April in 1966, a little over a year before the most major riots in Hong Kong's post-war history.

On Monday, one man had staged a hunger strike to protest the proposed Star Ferry fare increase. Patricia had seen the striker when she daydreamed on the bus and overshot her stop by one. "Are things that bad?"

"I hope not." But he looked worried. As a civil servant, the Senior Dispenser to the Chief Pharmacist, he preferred to believe the governor wouldn't let things get out of control. He returned to reading his newspaper.

At recess that morning, the playground buzzed with talk of the protests. Wong Yin-Fei, her best friend, was adamant. "It *is* expensive if you have to cross the harbor to work every day." She was a tall girl, of athletic build, a lifeguard, champion swimmer and leader of the basketball team as well as the Orchids' PL, as patrol leaders were known.

Patricia, who was on the swim team only because Yin-Fei coerced her, said. "But it's illegal to demonstrate. Can't they talk things out? This has been brewing for months. Those in charge ought to pay more attention before things get this bad."

"It's that *gwaipo,* Mrs. Elliot," their classmate Teresa chimed in. "My brother says it's her fault, stirring up the workers."

"That's rubbish. Elsie Elliot gets the government to listen to the workers *because* she's English, like them." Yin-Fei was shouting now, her long arms flailing wildly in the air. "Don't you see how unfair it is? The Star Ferry's a monopoly."

Teresa, who had only spoken to say something, didn't respond. She was thinking about the fashion show that Sister V, their headmistress, had agreed to hold, and the dress she was designing as her entry.

The bell rang, signaling the end of recess. Patricia tried to calm her friend. Yin-Fei's father, Dr. Wong, taught politics at the university and loved to debate. Any time Patricia went over to their home, he would ask her opinion about all sorts of subjects in the same excitable manner Yin-Fei exhibited.

This whole business was absurdly complicated.

On their way back to class, Patricia asked. "Hey, are you worried about this afternoon?"

Yin-Fei was surprised. "The protestors won't bother you."

"Not that. Maria."

"Oh, that. I told my patrol to vote for Maria, and you told your Snowdrops didn't you? The Forget-Me-Nots are bound to go for her since she is their PL. That's three out of four. Majority wins, right, right?" Her voice rising to its high-pitched cackle, she poked Patricia, hard, in the ribs. "Besides, the Violets won't dare vote differently."

"It's not the Violets I'm worried about," she replied, rubbing her side. Sometimes, she wished Yin-Fei would be a little less physical.

They arrived at the classroom where their teacher frowned at them, the last two stragglers, and they hurried to their seats in silence.

After history class that afternoon, Maria came by. She was furious. "Sister V says all after school activities have to be cancelled. Do you know what that means?"

Louis Philippe's pear-shaped body bounced around Patricia's imagination. Kings, she decided, couldn't look ridiculous if they wanted to be taken seriously. "What?"

"Aren't you listening to me? Sister V says . . ."

"I heard you. It's because of the trouble." She adjusted her glasses which had slid down her nose. As usual, Maria looked impeccable. Her royal blue Guides' uniform was starched and pressed, the yellow tie properly knotted, black shoes shined and hair neatly tucked under the navy beret. Her brass trefoil gleamed. Shining anything was not Patricia's strong suit.

Maria scowled, hands on her hips. "But we're voting today."

Patricia stared at her former PL. Her stomach ached. Maria

stood slightly shorter than her; stocky and tough, she was built like a fighter. "There's nothing we can do. We'll just have to wait a week. Besides, you're going to be CL anyway."

"Did you do your best to make sure?"

Uncomfortable, Patricia shifted her gaze towards the two, white cloth stripes sewn on her friend's pocket, the PL symbol. Maria had once been the older girl she idolized, the one who taught her everything when she was a novice. Did a third stripe mean that much to her? "Of course. Everyone knows you're it. This vote thing's just for show. Like we said it was," she added, tentatively.

"You don't even care!" Maria shrieked, so loudly that several girls in the corridor stopped to stare. "You didn't even bother wearing your uniform today. You smart girls are all alike," she said before storming off.

Patricia was nauseated. All she wanted was to go to bed and forget the day. How had things gotten so out of hand?

On the bus home, she reflected guiltily on the state of her life. The real trouble began a month ago when Maria brought up the idea of a CL to Captain, their adult advisor, a former student who led their Company. "They have them in England," Maria said, proving she'd done her homework. All the PL's agreed, expecting Captain to appoint Maria, who, as the most senior, deserved the post.

Captain had other ideas. "We'll let the Company decide. You nominate candidates who have to campaign, and we'll vote. Majority wins."

Maria had been stunned. Patricia quickly spoke up. "But Captain, you've always appointed our leaders. Why change things now?"

"Sometimes, change is inevitable," Captain said. "Sister V did suggest we consider elections. You vote for a president at school, don't you? This is the same thing."

There was no arguing with Captain once she'd made up her mind.

A year earlier, Sister V had abolished the system of prefects and head girl appointed by teachers, and instituted a student government and elections. *Self-determination increases social responsibility,* she claimed. Anyone, even a first former could run, although none dared since all the girls believed only upper formers were qualified to lead, despite what Sister said. Maria had written it off and refused to vote. "Such *fukjaahp* foreign methods," she scoffed, "these American nuns really make things complicated, don't they?" Yin-Fei had been intrigued, and borrowed a book from the library on the U.S. government. When Patricia asked why, she shrugged in her usual way. "You never know, it might be useful someday," but when pressed to run, said she wasn't ready. Yin-Fei did, however, campaign for the sixth former who won the presidency. Patricia voted but hadn't known what to make of it all.

Maria's accusation nagged. It wasn't fair. Patricia did care; she hadn't spent four years in the Company for nothing. Just because she brought her uniform to change into instead of wearing it to school . . . even her boyfriend Melvin said there wasn't any reason to be conspicuous, and he was in the Boy Scouts. Besides, she was beginning to find Guides a little childish. Only why did she feel so awful?

By evening, an air of protest filled the streets of Tsimshatsui where she lived.

At dinner, her father was annoyed. "The truth of the matter," he declared, "is that the government doesn't listen to what people say until it's too late." His statement startled her. Her father rarely commented on politics. It was the first time she'd ever heard him criticize his employer.

Yin-Fei rang later. "Guess what? I'm going to demonstrate in sympathy for that hunger striker with some of my dad's students."

"Are you nuts? It'll be dangerous out there." Patricia peered out of her twelfth floor window overlooking Nathan Road. "There's not a whole lot going on down below at the moment that I can see."

"It'll get bigger, you'll see. Hey, got to go. Tell you all about it tomorrow."

Seconds later, Melvin rang. He was worried. "Don't go out tonight, especially in your area."

"I wasn't planning to," she replied, peeved at his presumption. "Yin-Fei's going to stand vigil, you know."

He wrinkled his nose. "She would."

"Why shouldn't she?"

"You always defend her even when she's wrong."

Patricia bristled but was too tired to argue. "Well, talk to you later."

"Okay, bye."

Strictly speaking, he *wasn't* her boyfriend although . . . that too was becoming difficult. From the corner of the living room, the radio crackled with news of disturbances in the streets.

It's democracy, Captain had said when announcing the new selection process for CL. *You girls should learn to make your own choices.*

Patricia drew the venetian blinds.

What was the *matter* with everything anyway? Had the whole world gone utterly and completely mad?

Not madness but a necessary chaos, Patricia's university thesis contended. After that time, there was no turning back.

In the autumn of '96, Dr. Patricia Chow said. "The late sixties were watershed years. By 1966, people wanted control over their lives after the run on the banks the year before. Affordable public transport was important to survival, especially then, when Hong Kong was poorer. You know the saying. What are the four essentials? *Yi, sihk, jyuh, hahng.* Without clothing, food, shelter and transport, life can't begin."

A girl raised her hand. "Is that like Maslow's hierarchy?"

"In a way." Patricia appreciated the question — these university kids asked so few — but wished it had been less tangential. Her students didn't find their own history relevant. All they cared about was getting a job and making lots of money. She couldn't blame them though. Competition was stiff these days because graduates returned in droves from abroad with their foreign degrees now that the economy at home was stronger than in the West.

The hour and a half was up. She handed out the assignment

for the course and dismissed the class. The Maslow student lingered. It was the first week of term and Patricia didn't know the group.

"Dr. Chow? Why do we have to spend so much time on 1966?"

Patricia removed her glasses. How oddly challenging she was. "Don't you find it interesting?"

"Well yes, of course, and I'm sure it's important, but the whole April 5th thing seems like such an isolated political incident. Shouldn't we learn about longer term government policy developments?"

Patricia frowned. The title of her seminar was "Significant Moments in the History of Hong Kong." She responded, a trifle testily. "This isn't a survey course."

"Uh huh." The girl seemed thoughtful. "Anyway, this paper you want us to write, researching one incident, well I feel it would be more significant to cover a broader topic, like the growth of trade."

Patricia felt the start of a migraine. Lately, students were quite impossible

"It's an excellent research topic," the student persisted.

She glanced at her watch. "I'm sure it is. Why don't you think about it and we'll discuss the papers next time, okay?"

"Thanks Dr. Chow!"

Afterwards, a colleague offered coffee in the faculty lounge. Patricia mentioned her student. He scratched his chin. "That wouldn't be our 'growth of trade' girl, would it?"

"You *know* her?"

"She signed up for my course on the downfall of the Qing

dynasty last term and insisted on submitting her 'growth of trade research paper.'"

Patricia laughed. "What did you do?"

"I didn't have to do anything. She disappeared from my class after the first day."

At the second session, Patricia elaborated on her expectations for their papers. It was a lecture she gave every term. "Go to the newspaper archives. Dig up the facts and read about how things were. Ask your parents or grandparents. Recent history is oral. It's captured in the memories of ordinary life. If you don't bother to find out, who will?"

The Maslow student had not disappeared. After class, she brought up her paper again.

"My point is," she said, "we can't write papers on moments because there isn't enough information."

"But you haven't even looked." Patricia responded.

"So if I look and still don't find it, can I write about the growth of trade?"

Patricia tried to concentrate on what the girl was saying, but her face got in the way. There was something peculiarly familiar about those features. The wide mouth, bad complexion and slightly crooked nose. And that intent, almost ferocious expression. She didn't reply.

The girl was still speaking. "And if I find it within my area of interest? Can I use my topic then?"

"Perhaps," she conceded, "if you focus on an incident or piece of legislation or something that was pivotal. Do your research first and present an abstract."

For a moment, the student looked as if she were about to argue further. Without another word, she stalked away.

The next morning, while brushing her teeth, it dawned on Patricia. Girl Guide Maria! That was who the girl resembled. She hadn't thought of Maria in years. She continued brushing absent-mindedly. Her gums bled when she rinsed.

At the quarterly dinner with her former schoolmates that evening, Patricia asked. "Whatever happened to Maria Cheung?"

These gatherings had been going on some sixteen years now. The largest had been a three-table dinner, the year a dozen girls returned from Vancouver simultaneously. The last couple of years were lively. With the handover to China only months away, people wanted to be around history in the making, and the ones who lived overseas kept dropping in for visits. Patricia almost missed this one because of a department meeting which had luckily been cancelled at the last minute.

Yin-Fei balanced a chunk of pepper-and-salt chicken between her chopsticks. A shred of red pepper fell on her sleeve. "No idea. She vanished. Years ago, I tried to call her when I first got back from the States, but her old number was some Pong family, I think." She popped the deep-fried golden piece into her mouth.

"Didn't she come to the Guides reunion? The year Captain visited? Too bad I was out of town." Patricia's eyes savored the chicken. Running her tongue over her still tender gums, she knew she should skip it. The aroma, however, was irresistible and she surrendered.

"No, I don't think so. She wouldn't anyway. She hated

Captain."

"That's a bit overstated."

"You think so? The girl was vicious."

"You should talk."

Another schoolmate showed up and the screech of greetings ensued. Frightening how much like teenage girls they still were. Patricia glanced at Yin-Fei's animated face. Her friend never changed. Maybe she'd gained a little weight, but at forty-six, that was understandable. Hard to believe she led the Free Hong Kong Party, appearing regularly in the media, meeting often with the governor and other top officials. Where had time flown?

"Hey you all," Yin-Fei was saying, "I'll need your support in my run for office. Most of you are in my district." Her head bobbed a count round the table.

"*Wei!* No talking politics. I don't want to get indigestion." Teresa, the fashion designer, was almost as loud as Yin-Fei. She launched into a monologue about her wildly successful show in Milan.

Patricia's attention wandered. Recently, she was constantly fatigued. Dreadful how sedentary she'd become. She really ought to exercise, or swim, perhaps. If not for teaching, she'd hardly be on her feet.

After dinner, Yin-Fei suggested ice cream. Patricia demurred, saying Melvin would be waiting, and that there was her kids' homework to consider.

"Tell that Melvin you were engaged in important political activities. Keep him waiting now and then. It'll raise your net worth." Yin-Fei let off her noisy cackle of a laugh. People on the streets of Central stared.

"Shh! You'll scare off your constituents," Patricia said, laughing, but she followed the group to the Haagen Daas in Lan Kwai Fong.

In between conversations, she asked. "Where do you suppose Maria ended up?"

Yin-Fei dug out a huge spoonful of banana split. "She didn't go to university. Probably the police or something. That thing for uniforms she had was kind of kinky."

"You're exaggerating," she replied, amazed at how much her friend ate.

"Why are you asking anyway?"

The face of the Maslow student flashed. "Oh, you know how it is when we get to our age. I wish she'd stayed in touch."

"She would if she wanted to. In the end, people do what they want, regardless. Right, right?" She tapped Patricia's shoulder lightly. "Besides, there's no changing history. You more than anyone should know. But listen, I'll need your help at the university, and Melvin's too. The Director of Hospitals has influence. You will help, won't you?"

"You know we will." There were times Patricia wished her friend would just get married and settle down.

But Maria. Since this morning, memories of Maria plagued her. If only . . . but perhaps Yin Fei was right. Some moments in history were better forgotten.

On her way home, however, she couldn't help remembering.

When Captain had insisted on at least two candidates for a new CL, hence stymieing their first line of resistance, Patricia's

Patrol Second had caught all the leaders off guard by nominating her. Later, away from Captain, Maria lost her temper, unreasonably so, Patricia felt, and only calmed down when Yin-Fei suggested what they all agreed to: Patricia would simply have to lose.

After school the next day, she stopped by Maria's homeroom because they planned to discuss things further. Patricia disliked being around the fifth formers; they were too cogent a reminder of her future School Cert, that dreaded public exam.

The teacher was scolding Maria.

"You're not going to pass if you skip the mock exams. It's imperative that you practice. You only get so many make up chances."

Unmoved, Maria said. "It can't be helped. I can take the test myself, without an inviglator. I won't cheat. As you know, my grandmother's sickly and sometimes I have to look after her."

"I know that." The teacher sounded resigned. "But you need to think about your future. If you want extra help, stay after school and I'll work with you."

"That's impossible. There's Guides and . . ."

"Maria, stop making excuses!" She slammed a book so hard on the desk it flew to the floor. "That's only extracurricular. You're old enough to know what's important. Do you want to fail and repeat another year?"

Maria appeared unfazed. "Well, I have to get back home and cook dinner. Both my parents work, you know. In a *factory*." The scorn in her voice was unmistakable.

From the doorway, Patricia marveled at the exchange. She

would never dare speak to any teacher that way. Maria was so sure of herself she confronted those in charge. It was admirable. Other girls capitulated to authority even when they didn't agree.

Of course, Maria wasn't like everyone else. She was one of the few girls who lived in the public housing estates. Her religious conversion, not her grades, had enabled her to attend their government subsidized Anglo-Chinese Catholic school. Patricia had been to her home once, three years ago, and the sight shocked her. It was a one hundred square foot flat which housed all six of her family. Communal toilets and cold water taps were down the corridor, shared by a dozen other units. Her own home, a seven hundred square foot private flat for three people, was luxurious by comparison. After that time, she never again questioned why schoolwork was insignificant to Maria.

Maria brightened on seeing her. "So," she demanded, "how will you 'campaign' since it's 'our first election, how exciting.'" She spoke in English, her accent mocking Captain's less than fluent Cantonese. *"Gwaipo.* They're all the same," she grumbled, reverting to Cantonese. "She just wants to look good in front of Sister V."

How unfair, Patricia thought. Although the leaders often disagreed with Captain, her being foreign had nothing to do with anything. None of the Chinese teachers were willing to be their adult leader, claiming they hadn't any experience. This Portuguese bank teller had volunteered, keeping the Company going for over ten years. "Captain doesn't have to impress Sister. It's not like the school pays her."

Maria linked Patricia's arm in her own. "Forget that. Tell me, what will you propose? If you help me, I'll be prepared with arguments against your plans."

"I'm not sure yet." The truth was, she had avoided thinking about it. Although she'd agreed to the scheme, the whole idea defied logic. How could she come up with a deliberately bad program and present that seriously?

"You *are* going to do this the way we agreed, aren't you?"

Maria's tone irritated her. Why did she have to be so insistent? "I don't let my friends down."

"Make sure you don't, promise?"

"Of course."

She shook Patricia's arm. "Show me. On your honor."

Patricia raised the three-fingered salute, surprised at her own reluctance. "Honor."

The ice cream worried Patricia's stomach, and she regretted, once again, having given into Yin-Fei, who possessed a cast iron digestive tract.

Her daughters were already asleep when she got home. Melvin was up.

"Where were you?"

"With Yin-Fei and the others. You know how we are when we get talking."

Her husband returned to his magazine. He was peeved, Patricia knew, because he had had to deal with their girls' homework on his own. Tonight though, she simply couldn't concern herself with him. Besides, he would have forgotten by morning.

In the bathroom, she took some Pepto Bismol and ran water for a bath. The problem of Maria nagged, forcing its way back.

When Captain had announced the count, it took a minute before Patricia realized she'd won. Most of 19th Kowloon turned out to vote. The one absentee was Maria's Second, who claimed she had a cold. Patricia suspected otherwise. The girl was too embarrassed to show, probably because she guessed the outcome.

It was a clear majority, 25 to 9.

Maria blinked, disbelieving. Then, her moment of horror vanished, quickly replaced by apparent indifference. Catching Yin-Fei's eye, Patricia nodded, hoping she would understand and go to Maria immediately afterwards. The clamor of congratulations went on, it seemed, forever. By the time everyone scattered, the only PL left was the Violets girl, and she was on her way out.

Dusk blanketed the school.

Checking first in the bathroom, Patricia felt stupid. They wouldn't go where *anyone* might come in. They had to have gone some place private. Of course, the primary school! Maria had the key to the side door because she ran the Brownies' Pack. Their wooden toadstool and other paraphernalia were kept in a closet there.

The door was ajar. Maria was sobbing. Patricia didn't go in.

"All they care about is boys. Here I've presented the best program in the world, and they don't appreciate it. See what happens when you let the ignorant choose."

"Come, it's not so bad," Yin-Fei consoled.

"And Captain! How could she allow such a thing? All

because of that stupid Sister V. Why does she have to stick her nose into our business? It's got nothing to do with her. Our Company belongs to its own district. We can break away from the school if we want."

Yin-Fei laughed gently. "Yes, but then we wouldn't have any members."

"Oh, be serious." Maria wept, unstoppable, as if her heart were broken.

Patricia's eyes moistened. It was all too bad. Perhaps if the other three leaders went to Captain, they might get her to change . . . but she knew: that wasn't an option anymore. Before "Taps" this evening, Captain said that minority voices always had a right to be heard; in fact, she encouraged them never to be afraid to voice any opinion. However, Patricia had won fairly, and the company must now abide by this decision.

She was about to go in when she heard her name.

"And that Patricia," Maria said. "She doesn't know anything about leadership. Imagine promising 'more activities with the Scouts'! I know you're friends with her, but frankly, she's wishy-washy. The girls voted for her because she'll organize parties and isn't strict. They know she'll do whatever they want. Oh, it just isn't fair."

"Calm down. Let's get some ice cream, my treat, okay?"

The sobbing subsided and Patricia heard a rustle of the gathering up of things. She left before they emerged.

That evening her mother asked whether or not she was ill and why wasn't she eating her favorite chicken dish? When Melvin called afterwards, she said she'd won but that it didn't mean anything. He replied that everything meant something.

Night fell. Patricia sat up in bed, unable to sleep.

Her first thought, after she'd found those two, was to tell them she would resign. But then Maria had said what she did, and Yin-Fei didn't even object. She *wasn't* wishy-washy! Hadn't she pushed her girls to challenge themselves by taking those badges few attempted, like reader or commonwealth knowledge? It made more sense than knot tying, rope throwing, tent pitching and ten-mile hikes — especially the hikes — which excluded all but the most physically fit girls. Girls like Maria. As a new PL, Patricia had wanted to have fun with the Snowdrops. They did too, building the best campfires for parties, and buying firewood at the lowest price per catty. They were friends even beyond Guides. Friendship struck her as more important than the Company.

She had challenged her Second after the nomination, wanting to know why she wasn't asked. The younger girl replied defiantly. "We knew you wouldn't let us."

"But Maria's the most qualified to lead. You know that."

Her Second hesitated, struggling with what she wanted to say. "Maria only wants to do things she likes. That's not what a leader should do. You're different. You care about us. Besides, you're always telling us to do what we think is right. *This* is right."

During the days before the election, a number of girls from other patrols told her she had their vote. No, she'd said to every single one, vote for Maria. You know she's your real leader. Many giggled and didn't say anything, but a few said no, that wasn't their opinion.

The splash of water against her leg startled her. The tub was overflowing. She turned off the tap, distressed by the mess at her feet.

Tonight, Yin-Fei had confided that winning might be tough. "People hold my green card against me. Seems I'm not 'local' enough," she snorted.

"Would you give it up?"

"Probably. I won't lose without a fight. Even if I win though, it's not like we'll get popular support for challenging Beijing. It's likely my party will have to. In the long run, we'll be in the minority."

"So why are you doing this?" Patricia demanded.

"Once the British leave, isn't it up to us to at least try? Someone has to, and we are the lucky ones."

"Are we? Since when was life fair?"

Her friend shrugged. "You're always too philosophical. The trouble with us smart girls is that either we think too much or do too much. We should just make money like Teresa and jet around to Milan and Paris. Right, right?" Her laughter rang into the night.

In her last TV appearance, Yin-Fei said that the lifestyle and freedoms Hong Kong had would erode unless people acted to keep them. This was their home. If they didn't care about their society, who else would? After all, in the eyes of the Chinese government, democracy was merely a relic of an unjust treaty, leftover by colonial rulers who disregarded the true desires of the majority.

Patricia stepped into her bath. The warmth prickled her legs and thighs as she lowered her body carefully into the tub.

When she'd presented her campaign proposal for CL, she had tried to make a joke of things by bringing up the Scouts, which made all the girls laugh. The truth of the matter, although she'd never admit it to anyone, not even now to Yin-Fei or Melvin, was that she had always secretly been glad she won. Maria's losing hadn't been her or anyone's fault. It was just what was meant to be.

Her husband tapped on the door to say he was going to bed, adding that their older girl had asked whether or not she should run for student government. He had said yes.

Her stomach began to settle. The steam wrapped its way around her, erasing this day. Patricia closed her eyes. She really must watch her diet from now on.

CRITICAL READING GUIDE

by **Mike Ingham**

How to get the most out of your reading of these stories.

Think about the following aspects of the each of the stories. Whether you are reading the stories as a reading circle or group or as a secondary/tertiary English class, ask yourselves some basic questions about each of the stories.

1 Genre? – Is it tragic, comic, satirical, realistic, etc.

2 Cultural context? – What cultural aspects of behavior and attitude inform the action of the characters in the story? How does the social and cultural setting affect the telling of the story and determine how characters act?

3 Theme(s)? – What ideas or social/political/psychological/ philosophical points are made by the story?

4 Narrative voice/point of view? – Whose point of view is used for mediating the story? Would it be very different if the narrative were controlled by another voice?

5 Character(s)? – Are the characters merely a mouthpiece for the author's views and experiences, or do they have a convincing life of their own?

6 Language and style? – How do language and style affect our response to the story? What effects are created by placing language and style in the foreground, so that the reader has to take notice of it, instead of taking it for granted?

7 Your own personal response to the story? Like/dislike? Why?

Personal response and personal interpretation and construction of meaning are quintessential in modern theory about literature. Trust your own intuition and personal response, because no two people will ever respond in exactly the same way to a work of art.

Advice to teachers/students:
Research the context background of these stories to some extent before you ask students to read them. Ask students to note interesting expressions or challenging vocabulary, especially italicized words. In class you could try to elicit the meaning of some of these loan words (borrowed from other languages) by asking students to guess from the context if they can. Remind students of the rich composite and very hybrid nature of the English language and the enormous influence that other languages have had on it during its evolution.

For follow-up activities discussion and debates on the events, themes and topics of the story are always a source of language development, and encourage the students to see the connection between literature and life. In general, the relationship between fact and fiction is central to the collection. Students can be asked to collect their own Hong Kong stories, which blend fact and fiction. They can use their own experiences and those of their family members as raw material. These stories could be collated and published for internal or external readership by students. Encourage them to think about the way the story is told, and especially the point of view. After reading stories that seem particularly suitable for dramatic treatment (e.g. Until the Next Century, Chung King

Mansion) the students can dramatize them – either for live performance, or video/audio recording. Script-writing will really help them to appreciate and understand how narrative and dialogue really work in stories, such as those in this collection by Xu Xi.

History's Fiction

Hong Kong stories from the last four decades – i.e. from the sixties to the nineties. History and fiction (i.e. fact and fiction) merge and are blurred in the representation of Hong Kong life, (e.g. the Star Ferry riots, the Tiananmen massacre, the 1997 Handover) provide background color and authenticity. There is a strongly feminist orientation in a number of the stories (often subtly underlaid in the subtext), e.g. Until the Next Century; The Tryst; Democracy, as well as a concern with evaluating socio-political events from the perspective of ordinary people. Many of the stories in Xu Xi's collection move seamlessly between past and present, employing frequent time-shifts (flashback and flashforward), in order to emphasize the causal relationship between time present and time past. ('Time present and time past / Are both perhaps present in time future, / And time future contained in time past.' See T.S. Eliot's poem "Burnt Norton" which opens his *Four Quartets*).

Nineties

Until the Next Century: Conclusion to long-running affair between rich, Beijing-born businessman and independent-minded Hong Kong woman. Setting: her Hong Kong flat. Explores issue of *qingfu's* (love-wife or extra-marital lover) status, but from a more feminist perspective. 'She' is more independent and self-reliant than 'he' is. The narration is from a third-person perspective, which gives the story's focus on detail (e.g. the jacket on the chair and the wine-glass) a film-like quality.

Focus Questions

1 Why do you think the author opted to name her minor characters in this story but not her two main characters?
2 Why is the story structured as a series of flashbacks (like many films)? Would it work equally well if it had been told in a chronological sequence from beginning to end?
3 What is the significance of New Year's Eve as a thematic motif in the story?

Follow-up Activities

1 Write a brief summary of the story from the man's viewpoint. Imagine he is telling his best friend or brother about the long-running affair on New Year's Day 2000.
2 Write a short 'goodbye scene' between two people, which takes place on New Year's Eve. Choose a suitable setting.

Insignificant Moments in the History of Hong Kong: An experience of the two days – June 30 and July 1st 1997, which saw the return of Hong Kong to Chinese sovereignty. The rather mundane experiences of Yam Kuen and his Uncle Cheuk – both working in the service industries, the former in a smart club and the latter in a small restaurant under the Central escalator – are contrasted implicitly and to some extent ironically with the more 'significant' experiences of the more important players and the other ordinary Hong Kong folk. Unlike them, uncle and nephew have to work. Casual talk of the restaurant cat that is afraid of mice is a whimsical and ironic reference to Deng Xiao Ping's famous analogy to explain the differences between the Chinese political system and the Hong Kong one under the One Country Two Systems scheme.

Focus Questions

1 Why do you think the story is about insignificant historical moments rather than significant ones? What does the writer appear to be saying about Hong Kong's momentous date with history?

2 What function does the children's story about the white rabbit and the moon have in the story? What does it suggest about different perceptions and ways of seeing things? How is it connected with the two main characters? Is it seen as a positive omen of the future?

3 Why do you think the author prefaced the story with the cat quotation by Deng Xiao Ping?

Follow-Up Activity

Write your own diary account of a significant day in your life. Write another diary entry about an insignificant day for you, which coincides with an important day for others or for local/national/world events – e.g. 9/11; the Christmas tsunami; or the Hong Kong Handover.

Blackjack: Stream of consciousness monologue about uncertainties of living 'astronaut' life – between Hong Kong and the U.S.A. References to Hong Kong handover. Life is seen as a series of gambles, where the outcome is uncertain. Setting: Atlantic City casino just prior to 1997 and Hong Kong MTR exit to Tsimshatsui.

Focus Questions

1 The story seems to function on oppositions, contrasts and paradoxes. Can you identify some of them?

2 What do you think is the significance of the italicized words in the text? Try to work out their meanings and relate them to the themes of the story and the character of the narrator.

3 'Multinational city. A make-believe world deliberately reminiscent of Shanghai.' Do you think this is an accurate description of Hong Kong, or an outdated one?

4 Why does gambling figure so prominently in the action and imagery of this story? How is it connected to the references to 1997 and the Hong Kong Handover

Follow-up Activity

Write a short passage about a journey back after a long absence to the place, where you (or your narrator) were born. Describe the mood and sensations you experience on the first day.

Eighties

Manky's Tale: Man-Kit (Manky) returns from the U.S.A. to Hong Kong, leaving his Hong Kong-born wife Rosa M. behind in the States, in order to be with his dying father. From the background sound of the radio in his father's hospital room he becomes conscious of the Hong Kong protest marches in the aftermath of the Tiananmen massacre. Setting: Hong Kong, early summer, 1989. Read "Danny's Snake" in the same author's collection, *Daughters of Hui* — and re-read this one. They are companion stories, and complement each other effectively.

Focus Questions

1 Why do you think the author switches to a male first-person narrator in this story? Normally her protagonists are female. Is Manky's character well depicted and convincing? State your opinion.

2 How does the story present the reader with a confused sense of cultural identity on the part of the narrator? Can this in any way be seen as representative of other people's identity confusion in Hong Kong? State your view.

3 Show how jazz and musical references are important to the story's style and theme.

4 Why do you think the author chooses to make only indirect references to the Tiananmen Square massacre of 1989, which had such strong repercussions in Hong Kong? Why doesn't she amplify this background detail and place it in the foreground of the story?

Follow-Up Activity

Find out from the internet and books/documentaries about the events of June 4 1989 in Beijing. Can you find any other writings that refer to these events?

The Fourth Copy: This story is a good example of meta-fiction — that is, a story about story-writing. Grace Hsu wishes to be taken seriously as a writer, and finds inspiration in her school experiences for a novel she is writing. She has moved to New York in 'the land of liberty' to escape the straitjacket of her Hong Kong identity and the memories of her traumatic past – 'One interracial marriage. One divorce. One attempted rape by a colleague. One abortion. One suicide attempt. Just the typical adventures of the average self-proclaimed feminist of the latter part of the twentieth century from a part of the world where feminism isn't 'necessary'.'

Focus Questions

1 What is the significance for the story of the passages in italics? Why does the author use italics for these sections, do you think?

2 Why is the phrase 'not the thing, but the perception of the thing' important to our understanding of the theme of the story?

3 The story (and Grace herself) plays with the idea of various possible endings. How effective is the ending that the author chooses? Is Grace merely being ironic about 'living happily ever after in the castle'?

Follow-up Activity

If Grace's narrative were extended to a novel or novella length story, how do you think it might be developed? Write a brief synopsis of your ideas.

Discuss — To what extent are stories and poems autobiographical? Is it more authentic when we write about ourselves, or can we write about others and imaginary worlds with conviction? Try to think of some examples.

Rage: An unnamed narrator reminisces on a bittersweet love affair with a charming but spoilt youngest son. The setting is both Hong Kong and New York. The interior monologue technique addresses the self as 'you', so that the structure and tone of the story seem dialogic – talking mentally to oneself! The technique implies both self-blame and, at the same time, an ability to face up to one's emotional and sexual instincts, which are stronger than rational argument or common sense behavior.

Focus Questions

1 Why do you think the author has chosen the second-person form (you) as the narrative subject?

2 Can you think of another story in the collection that has an unnamed central couple? Does this story have anything in common with it?

3 This story is basically a sequence of memories. Why do you think 'the rage erupts' at the end?

4 Show how the Hong Kong context is lightly sketched to provide a backdrop for this story. (You may need to do a little research).

Follow-Up Activity

Invent a character who talks to herself/himself about a frustrating situation vis-à-vis a relationship. Write a short monologue in which the character 'lets off steam' or vents her/his rage.

Seventies

The Yellow Line: A nameless housing estate boy from Lok Fu discovers an alternative Hong Kong existence in nearby Kowloon Tong just after the opening of the MTR in 1979. His addiction to traveling on the 'underground iron' is stronger than his awareness of his own social 'station' (excuse the pun!). His glimpse at the world of the more privileged international school-boys of St George's, contrasted with the misery of domestic life in his own dysfunctional family, has tragic consequences (as implied by the final paragraphs of the story.)

Focus Questions

1 Despite being told in the third person (omniscient narrative viewpoint) the reader is able to imagine the boy in the story's thoughts and impressions about the MTR, the richer people in Kowloon Tong, the foreign schoolchildren at the international school, etc. Find some examples in the story of this 'free indirect speech' which puts the child's curious questions directly into the narrative itself. Why do you think this device is useful for this particular story?

2 Why do you think the writer has the boy commit suicide at the end of the story? Does it seem as if he is really committing suicide or leaping into another dimension or world?

Follow-Up Activity

Write an alternative ending to the story *either* in which the boy does not die *or* in which he enters a alternative existence (something like a fantasy story like Peter Pan).

Discussion — Has suicide by youngsters in Hong Kong been

covered up or played down by the authorities here. How can the problem be tackled more robustly and effectively?

The Tryst: First-person female narrator relates an unforgettable encounter with a strikingly self-possessed young French woman in Taipei and later Hong Kong. The Tryst (a word used to describe a lovers' meeting) is an assertive tale of female bonding, which explores issues of male-female and female-female relationships frankly and without taboo.

Focus Questions

1 How does the 'I' narrator's passivity (my passivity does not trouble me) affect the events that she recounts in the story? Ultimately is passivity seen as a positive or negative character trait, or neither?

2 Show how the use of French words creates a special ambience (atmosphere) that runs throughout the text. Give some examples from the story.

3 How is the fictional Hong Kong character Suzie Wong used as a reference point in the story? What image of Hong Kong is suggested by this character? Do you think she evokes an accurate image of the place?

Follow-Up Activity

Imagine that a film version of this story was due to be screened in your place of study, but that at the last moment the authorities had decided to ban it because of its 'immoral content'. Write a strong argument in defense of the story's artistic treatment of a topic that many conservative people are still very afraid of. Explain why the story has something valuable and relevant to say to a modern audience.

Sixties

Chung King Mansion: Recollections of narrator Ai-Lin's childhood in 1960s Tsimshatsui, which follow her fascination with an orange-haired young lady waiting for U.S. sailors outside Chung King Mansion. An atmospheric and accurate depiction of 1960s Tsimshatsui (with Nathan Road on the waterfront before seventies land reclamation moved it inland!), which presents the mundane truth and daily hypocrisies of adult life through the eyes of an innocent child, to powerful literary effect. Graham Greene's story "The Fallen Idol" treats a similar theme.

Focus Questions

1 What stylistic and linguistic devices are used to convey the idea of a child writing about her experiences as a child, rather than writing a memoir from the perspective of an adult? Mention some examples from the text. In your view does the story succeed in conveying the impression of a being a child's diary or personal journal

2 How does the author exploit the ironic humor of Ai Lin's innocence about sexual matters? Give some specific examples from the text.

3 'The story deals especially with the loss of innocence and cautions young people about having idols or icons.' Do you agree with this statement? Why/why not?

4 Why do you think the orange-haired girl remains an external character to the psychological action of the story. Why isn't the reader allowed to get closer to her?

Follow-Up Activities

Imagine that Ai-Lin gets into the lift with her orange-haired 'lady'. Write the dialogue of their meeting.

Write a short narrative about one of your own childhood experiences, in which location (milieu) features prominently to accentuate the authentic 'local color' of the story.

Democracy: The background of 1966-7 Hong Kong Star Ferry riots frames this allegorical tale about issues of small-scale and large-scale democracy among four convent-school, girl-guide friends, Patricia (whose point of view is primary), Yin-Fei (who later becomes a democracy activist in post-handover H.K.), Teresa (more clothes and fashion-conscious than the others) and Maria (the disappointed candidate from a poor housing estate family). This is a tale of competition, of challenge to preconceived attitudes and ideas and of mixed emotions among the increasingly politically-aware, upper-form students. It suggests implicit parallels between the mechanisms of smaller-scale and larger-scale democracy and also between the quality of democratic debate and practice in the 60s and present-day Hong Kong.

Focus Questions

1 'Without clothing, food, shelter and transport life can't begin.' To what extent are these four essentials more important than democracy in your view? Is such a view relevant to the events of this story? Why does Patricia describe the events of the period as 'a necessary chaos', do you think?

2 What analogies are drawn by the author between the political processes of small-scale democracy and the large-scale model?

3 To what extent do you think the adult lives of Patricia and her friends have been affected by the events surrounding the Girl Guide elections? What is the role of the retrospective view in this story, as compared with, say, Chung King Mansion?

4 Discuss the importance of factual historical background in the construction of this fictional narrative. Would the story work in the same way without the factual background?

Follow-Up Activities

Research the life and work of Elsie Tu (nee Elliott) OR the impact on Hong Kong past and present of the 1966/7 social disturbances.

Discussion — Is present-day democracy an improvement on the ideas of democracy in the past? Can true democracy be achieved in Hong Kong or in any other country e.g. the United States? What are the obstacles that stand in its way?

Mike Ingham came to Hong Kong in 1989, and has taught literature at the English department of Lingnan University since 1999. Previously, he worked for the Institute of Language at the Hong Kong Education Department. Speech development, literature and drama in education are his areas of expertise, and he is the founder member of Theatre Action, a Hong Kong drama group that specializes in action research on literary drama texts. Ingham also co-edited two anthologies of Hong Kong literature in English, *City Voices* and *City Stage*. He has a BA and masters degrees in European literature and linguistics from the University of Oxford, and a PhD in English drama and literature from the University of Hong Kong.